HOLD ON TO HER

OLIVIA STEPHEN

Best—
Olivia Stephe

Editor: Jenn Wood, https://allabouttheedits.wixsite.com/editingproofingbeta

Cover Designer: Alex Beeman

Cover models: Alexandra Davis, Alex Beeman

Formatting: Jessica Ames

To Mom and Dad,
I love you, always

Prologue

SARAH

Blood.
There isn't supposed to be this much blood.
Pain.
There isn't supposed to be this much pain.

Within seconds, I'm doubled over with cramps so intense, so dizzying, the thought of dying is at the forefront of my mind. It's a pain like no other. Like a vice tightening around my middle.

My arms rest on the edge of the toilet seat, holding me up before the next wave of nausea hits. More dry heaves.

Breathe in. Breathe out.

My eyes close again, the image of a beautiful baby girl surfacing. She's stunning with pale skin and shiny, green eyes.

I love you.

"Oh my God, Sarah! What's wrong? Jesus, you're bleeding, sweetheart." Mother's scream jars me awake. Her footsteps are hurried as she makes her way to me, dropping to her knees. She cradles me like an infant, rocking me back and forth. I won't get to hold my baby like this.

"It's gonna be okay, sweetheart. You're gonna be okay. I'm going to get the phone to call for an ambulance, okay?"

"I'm losing my baby." Four words whispered and many tears shed. Four simple words and endless tears that will, no doubt, change me forever. "Please help me."

So much blood. So tired.

I've lost Daniel. I'm losing my baby.

It's my last thought before the darkness consumes me.

Chapter One

SARAH

Six Years Later

Completely whacked.

That's all I can think when I rewind my brain to the last visit with my parents. I'm sitting here in the mid-town coffee shop, attempting to focus on the scent of freshly-brewed coffee and the blueberry muffins that have obviously just been pulled out of the oven, instead of how I bailed out of Mom and Dad's before my sister arrived. Not even the tinkering of the coffee machines or the hum of quiet conversation can keep my mind from revisiting that fiasco. Mom continues to act as though nothing of any importance happened where my ex, Daniel, is concerned. She talks to him every day when she goes to watch my niece, Londyn. Every time she tells me about one of his corny jokes, my insides churn. When she babbles on about how wonderful he is, and that his degree from Duke and his new job will take care of Sydnee and the baby for years to come, it's like she's chipping away at my heart, piece by piece. Yet she doesn't even realize how it affects me. Talk about head in the sand.

It's as though the past has been completely erased in her mind. But as long as big sister Sydnee is happy, that's all that matters to her.

The scowl on my face is going to become a permanent expression if I keep up these conversations with my mom. Anger boils up and the grip on my coffee cup nearly breaks it in two, and if the coffee cup doesn't break, I'm going to have my long, wavy brown hair in knots if I keep twisting it.

"You know that face is way too pretty to be wrinkled up in such a frown." The deep, sexy voice that belongs to Liam snaps me out of my temporary misery as he waltzes over to my table and makes himself at home in the chair across from me, leaning his elbows on the table and folding his hands together. My stomach drops a few notches when I look at the sweet male perfection that is Liam Reynolds. His deep-set eyes scan my face, searching for something, although I don't know what that would be.

"Hey. Didn't even see you come in."

"Obviously. Whatever you're thinking sure has got you twisted up. You're damn near ready to crack that coffee cup in half. You okay?"

My head says that I will be eventually, but my heart tells a different story altogether. So, I do what I've mastered over the last several years. Avoid.

"What are you up to today?" I ask.

See? Avoid. I get better and better all the time.

"Not much. On my way to the bar to meet with Cole and Zane. I saw your car parked outside, figured I'd stop. You still haven't answered my question," Liam prods, reaching over to take my hand. It makes me nervous when I think about how much I'm beginning to care for Liam, so I pull my hand back, wrapping it around the coffee cup, along with the other one. He's been such a great friend to me that I don't want to substantiate the feelings I have for him because all we'll ever be is friends. He has the all-American family, while mine is...well, whacked. He has such a caring heart, and mine is locked up tighter than Fort freakin' Knox.

"I'll be fine. Don't worry about me." *I'm not sure I'll ever be fine again.*

"Look. I'm here to listen. That's what friends do, yeah? You've listened to me complain about Cole and all his women for the past however many months, so let me return the favor. You always pretend everything is okay, but I think I know better." Besides the fact that he's tall, chiseled, and oh-so-easy-on-the-eye, he's also perceptive. So much so, he's beginning to notice my avoidance behaviors and call me out on my shit.

"You're making this into something that it's not, Liam. Sometimes visiting Mom is difficult, but I'm fine. Give me a day and I'll forget all about it." I'm doing my best to lie my way through this conversation, but I have a feeling Liam isn't buying it.

"So how about if I help you forget then. Let's go to dinner and maybe hit the movies afterward. I'll even let you pick the flick. What do you say?"

"I'd say that sounds like a date." I drag the coffee cup to my lips to take a sip of the warm drink, thinking of anything I can say to change the subject. I'd love to go on a date with Liam, but I know what will happen when my heart becomes invested in a relationship, and there is no way in hell I'll go through that again. Liam is total boyfriend material and I don't do the boyfriend thing. Besides, with the mood I'm in, I wouldn't want to stop at dinner and a movie. Getting lost in Liam would be a great way to forget.

"What if it is?" His shoulders shrug as if it's no big deal.

For a brief moment, I let my mind wander and daydream about what it would be like to date this man. He's been nothing but kind to me. He's compassionate, hard-working, and talented, and I believe I mentioned the delicious and sexy part before. But that's exactly what I thought about Daniel at the beginning of our relationship too, and what a disaster that turned out to be.

Sadly, I shove those thoughts to the back of my mind. I can't go there.

"I don't think so, Liam. Listen, I'm meeting Raina at the gym. I'll just work out my issues pounding the treadmill… running helps," I say light-heartedly, hoping he won't notice the sadness in my voice at turning him down.

"You're getting good at running, Sarah," he whispers as he stands to leave, but I hear every word.

I'm already good at running.

"Liam," I call out.

"Yeah?"

"I'll see you tonight at the pub?"

"Yep. That's what we do, right? Meet up at the pub." The tiny bell above the door of the coffee shop dings a little too loudly as Liam leaves without saying goodbye.

And I'm left sitting here...by myself. Again. But it's what I'm used to. The way it needs to be.

I grab my phone and shoot a text to Raina, telling her I'll meet her at the gym in fifteen.

Chapter Two

SARAH

"Liam will lose his mind, Sarah. My God, look at you!" Raina bounces on her tiptoes and all but screams when I emerge from the bathroom after getting myself ready for a girls' night out after our workout at the gym. I'm trying to convince myself I haven't put any extra time into my hair and make-up tonight, but it's useless. Deep down, I know I have, and I know exactly the one reason why. Liam. I hate that I upset him this afternoon, but I'm not sure how to navigate this friendship when there's an obvious attraction there. I'm getting the impression he wants more with me, but I just don't do *more*.

"Babe, I think Liam and I are really just friends, and maybe with benefits someday, but strictly friends. You do know my track record with the opposite sex, right?"

"Will you let that go? Every girl has had her heart broken a time or two, so you're no different. Just let him in. Not every man is a dick."

"I'm not worried about him *being* a dick. Just so long as he has a decent sized one," I joke, as I finish my last gulp of wine, while Raina nearly spits hers out. I think she's speechless. But it's true, though. I don't need a relationship. Just a man's…man parts, and I'm good. Problem is, I seem more attracted to Liam than I'm comfortable with, so I'm not quite sure I could ever do the one-night stand thing with him.

"You're hopeless." She rolls her eyes, grabs her purse, and opens my front door. "Let's go. We've got more wine to drink."

THE COLD NOVEMBER air stings the exposed skin on my back where my black top dips low as Raina and I hustle into Sam's. The scent of fried food and alcohol fills the air, and hearing the music as I stand just inside the doorway makes my stomach flop just a little. Why, all of a sudden, do I feel like this? Nothing has changed between Liam and me. But when I see him on the small elevated stage playing his acoustic guitar and singing, my heart suddenly skips a beat, and my breath seems to catch in my throat. His eyes close, losing himself in the music, and he looks gorgeous. I'm in serious trouble, I just know it. The other women sitting near the stage are every bit as captivated by him as I somehow seem to be recently. Or maybe it isn't all that recent. Maybe all this time hanging around him, forging a strong friendship, has softened me just a bit. Either way, a tinge of jealousy hits when I think of him with one of those other skanks. That's what I call the gaggle of bimbos that follows Liam and Cole everywhere they go.

When I hear the beginning of the next song, I freeze...my feet are cemented in place. It's a song I recognize far too well...Michael Ray's "Get to You." To hear Liam sing those lyrics is a punch to the gut. He has no idea why I run away from love.

My damn feet need to move. I need to shake off the sinking feeling that's overtaking me and focus on the bar, and the strong drink I may need tonight. I feel flushed, a little overcome with the sexiness that is Liam Reynolds, and the words he sings are like an arrow he shoots straight to my heart. It scares me to watch him stare right into my eyes as he sings that song. His face is expressionless. For a brief moment, there's a hint of sadness passing over his eyes, but I turn quickly to avoid seeing anything else.

Damn it.

I lean in, whisper to Raina, and make a dash to the bathroom where I splash a bit of cool water on my cheeks in hopes of getting my emotions back under control. My reflection in the mirror stares back, reminding me to keep a lockdown on my feelings. No feelings, no relationships, no more than two dates, which is code for no more than twice in the sack with any man.

Walking back toward the bar, I stop and smile at the sight before me.

"Hey, babe." Zane leans over the bar and lays a sensual kiss right on the puckered lips of my best friend. Those two are so in love. Jealous isn't a feeling I'm too familiar with, but right now, that's exactly how I feel, and it's confusing. This isn't me. I don't do relationships. So why the hell do I look at theirs and wish it was me?

A drink. That's what I need. "Zane, Jack and Coke please, easy on the Coke. And hurry," I say adamantly, taking my seat at the bar.

"Sweetie, what is wrong with you? Jack and Coke?" Raina uses her whisper voice as she sits next to me.

"I just need a drink. That's all."

"And hurry," I hear a deep, sexy voice whisper in my ear. "Isn't that what you said?"

My eyes close at the sound of his voice and it takes a

second for my breath to catch up with the rest of me. His scent drifts across my nose and I breathe it in slowly. No man has ever affected me quite the way Liam does, and what's scary is that he knows.

"Um…yes. Hurry. I'm thirsty…now," I reply, without even turning around. My chin lifts and my eyes focus straight ahead, feeling the need to regain some semblance of control. Liam's hand rests on the bar stool, brushing against my back, causing my cheeks to flush pink, and my heart to speed up. Again. I can feel his thumb rubbing back and forth, causing goose bumps to rise on my arms, and sparks begin to come to life. So much for control. I'm about ten seconds away from losing it.

He can't do this to me.

"You okay, babe?" comes the voice again, smooth like satin or silk, directly into my ear, so close the scruff on his chin brushes against my cheek. All I can think about is how it would feel on the insides of my thighs.

"Of course. Why wouldn't I be?" I turn and immediately come face to face with sex. Hot, sticky, sweet sex.

Jesus.

"Oh, I don't know. You seem a bit nervous. Maybe a little jumpy," he responds, a smirk playing with a full-fledged smile on his gorgeous face.

Asshole.

"I'm fine. Perfectly fine." I turn back around to face the bar, nose in the air, only to find Zane, both hands on the bar top, head down as he chuckles.

Asshole.

"Zane, fix my damn drink. And hur…I mean, now," I plead, with a hint of frustration in my voice. Perhaps embarrassment, as well. I swallow the lump in my throat in hopes of regaining some composure.

Liam plants himself on the barstool next to mine,

ordering his drink. "I'll have what this beauty is having. And *hurry*." Tonight is obviously irritate-the-hell-out-of-Sarah night because the three of them are having a blast at my expense.

"What is wrong with you? And do you need to sit so close?" my voice nervously cackles and cracks.

"One of these days, you're going to let me get closer than this, sweetheart. You're gonna stop running."

I'm stock-still for a minute and prepare to turn and let him have it, but all I see as I do is his firm, gorgeous ass as he walks away from me, Jack and Coke in hand. I stare at said ass as he catches up to Cole, the other part-owner of Sam's and second half of the Liam and Cole duo. My eyes stay glued to him as he talks with Cole and the two air-headed bimbos with him. I squint when I see bimbo number two leaning in far too close to Liam.

Swinging my head around with a huff, I catch sight of Raina glaring at me.

"What?' I grab my Jack and Coke and take a big swig, nearly spitting it out at the burn I didn't realize I would feel. It's a "match to gasoline" type burn, and it takes my breath away. I gasp, trying to pull oxygen into my lungs. Raina pats my back as she nervously calls out to Zane to get me some water.

"Shit! Are you okay?"

After the coughing and wheezing spell diminishes, I manage to get my voice back.

"Wow. That's, um, really good."

"Drink the water," she says, shaking her head and handing me a full glass. "And Zane, get that shit away from her." He dutifully takes the remainder of the drink and pours it out in the small sink behind the bar. Raina takes her seat beside me again as my breathing returns to normal and the fire down my throat is extinguished.

"You know, he's only ever been nice to you. I just don't see the harm in seeing where things go with him. He's clearly into you, and I can tell by the anger I see in your eyes when you watch him with Cole's harem, that you're a little into him too."

"Don't. Just don't. I'm not going there with you tonight. To be honest, you shouldn't go there *any* night. I don't need to be reminded of how screwed up my luck is with men."

"Then I won't say a word. However, I will tell you this. Not all men are Daniel."

Daniel. Just mention of his name and my blood boils. You'd think I'd be over it all by now. But no. I seem to have this burning desire to hang on to all the shit from my past like a reality show hoarder. I don't know if I'll ever be able to let it go because I'm not so sure I can think of anything more devastating than walking in on your boyfriend doing a little naked mattress dancing with your sister. On *my* mattress. That image is burned in my brain forever. So, let another guy get close to me? No fucking thank you. Men are good for one thing, and if I thought I wouldn't hurt Liam getting it, I'd be all over him. He is obviously too good of a guy to tap once or twice then kick to the curb. He deserves better than that. I'm not at all sure I could stop at once or twice with him anyway. That man is built to please.

"I'm not having this conversation. End of."

"Sarah, I'm just trying to help. You know that," she says apologetically.

"I'm fine. I don't need help. I just need to finish this water and get out of here." I empty the glass and grab my purse and jacket. After giving Raina a hug, I walk briskly to the main entrance and stop, my hand gripping the door handle like a vice, listening to Liam and Cole on stage. My head turns without my permission. He sits on his stool, fingers gently strumming the strings, looking directly at me, directly into my soul, as he sings Keith Urban's "Break on Me."

I won't let him get to me. I'm doing just fine without a man.

And I'll just keep telling myself that.

Over and over and over again.

Maybe one day, I'll actually believe it.

Chapter Three

LIAM

Stubborn.

So damn stubborn.

Too stubborn, or maybe afraid, to see that I want her. I've seen that look in my older sister's eyes before, when she was dumped by some douche who cheated on her. Sarah's been hurt and just the thought of that makes me want to hunt someone down and beat the shit out of him.

The bar is closing up, and because it's late, I've already sent Zane home with Raina so they can spend some time together. It's tough when she teaches during the day and he works in the evenings. But hey, I'm a stand-up guy like that.

I take one last walk around the bar, checking to see that everything's closed down, then stop at the barstool where Sarah had parked her fine ass earlier this evening. It's hard not to replay the scene with her on this stool just a few hours ago. The closer I got, the more nervous she became. Her body physically shivered which made me smile. There is an attraction there, I know it. I feel it because it's strong. One brush of my thumb across her smooth and delicate bare back had her so tense, and it had me so damn hard, I nearly came in my jeans like some teenage boy seeing a naked woman for the first time.

She's gun-shy.

But I'm a very patient man.

Looking down, I notice a slight glare of something on the floor. Reaching for it, I realize it's a driver's license, so I grab it to put behind the bar, knowing someone will be in after it tomorrow.

However, it appears, ladies and gentlemen, that I am in luck. Looking at the card, I see it belongs to one Sarah Witten. So, remember earlier when I mentioned that I'm a stand-up guy? Well, I need to get this back to Sarah tonight. After all, I'm part-owner and I want to keep my customers happy.

Quickly, I lock the back door and make my way to my muscle car, which sits in its usual spot behind the bar. I start it up, backing it out of the space, and head in the direction of Sarah's small house. Not leaving her house till morning is all I have on my mind right now. *Pretty Miss Sarah...I'm coming for you*. Perhaps literally.

SLOWING down to pull in her driveway, I take a minute to think about how I'd like this late evening to play out. Sarah's place is a quaint little house that looks exactly what I picture her living in. The small front porch light shines like a beacon and lights up her narrow driveway. There is a dim light on in what I think is her living room, so I knock gently on the wooden door adorned with a colorful wreath.

I am nowhere near prepared for what I see when the door opens.

Sarah.

Sweet, sexy, Sarah in a long, sleek pink robe, and she's

clutching a book with a half-naked man and woman on the front. My little spitfire is a romance novel lover. Why am I not surprised?

She's holding the top of her robe tightly around a full set of tits as she opens the door, eyes wide open in surprise at seeing me here at two thirty in the morning. She's surprised and I'm in complete shock. Jesus, she's gorgeous. No make-up, and hair pulled high in her head, giving me a glimpse of the soft, satiny skin on her neck that I'd like to be sucking right now. And licking. And peppering with kisses.

"Um, hey. So..." I'm fumbling over my words like a moron. *Pull your shit together.*

"Liam. What are you doing here so late?" she asks in a gentle and quiet voice, laying the book down on the stand by the doorway. She opens the door further, allowing the cool night air to creep in, and I get a full-on view of this woman, draped in pink satin and sex.

Shit. I'm in big trouble.

"Um. You, uh, must have dropped your driver's license on the floor of the bar. I found it when I was cleaning up. Guess you'll need it, huh." I manage to get all that out without sounding like too much of an idiot. I reach into my pocket and hand her the card, my fingers lightly grazing over hers as she takes it from me.

Sarah's deep, green eyes meet mine and I feel as though I could fall right in, lost forever. She smiles, showing me the sexiest little dimples on both cheeks. There is no doubt about it...this woman will be the death of me. I need a taste. Just one taste, like a man in the desert searching for just one sip of life-saving water. Desperate.

"Could I come in for a few minutes?"

"Liam, it's late. I was just getting ready to head up to bed. Maybe another time."

Shit. No, not another time. Now.

"Just for a few minutes. I have something I need to say, or ask, rather." She looks back inside the house for a brief moment and turns to face me again.

"Okay. Just for a minute, though. I have to get up early to run some errands." She hesitates, but steps back, allowing me inside.

It's unnerving how comfortable I feel in her home. Her style of decorating gives it a very relaxed and calming atmosphere. Dim lighting, soft colors, and a large overstuffed sofa and chair sit gracefully in front of a small gas fireplace that is throwing off some pretty good heat. In front of the fireplace, a soft, white cushioned rug adds to the cozy feel of her place.

"So, what's up?" she questions.

"I'm just gonna cut to the chase because I'm tired of waiting. I really like you, Sarah, and I think you know that. We have a lot of fun hanging out together."

"You're a really great friend, Liam. Of course, I like you." She offers a slight smile but her eyes turn away and her arms move to hug around herself.

"But..." I say, because I know it's coming.

"No buts. I just think we're better as friends. That's all." She's a shit liar. Her eyes are shifting, looking all around. They look everywhere but at me. She couldn't be any more transparent if she tried. Instead of dropping this whole conversation like I should, I push forward. My feet move slowly, allowing me a chance to see her reaction the closer I get.

I love what I see. Sarah's tits are pushed up with her arms wrapped around her waist and I can see her hardened nipples right through the smoothness of her robe. I reach out my hand slowly so I don't scare her away. Her beautiful green eyes widen and her breathing quickens in desperation as my hand makes contact with her skin. My thumb rubs small circles around her warm, pink cheeks, and her eyes close for a moment, her head tilting into my touch. A small moan escapes her mouth and when that sounds hits my ears, I am rock-fucking-hard.

"Just friends?" I whisper, leaning in to brush my lips against her neck, against the softest skin I've ever had the pleasure of touching. The only scent I can detect is a hint of lavender, not only from the small candle she has burning, but from the body wash she must use as well. It's addicting, and I don't think I'll ever get enough.

"You sure about that, babe?"

"I'm...uh. I don't know. You're too close."

"Am I? Is that a bad thing?"

"Just, you know..." Her eyes close as she unwraps her arms from her mid-section, bringing her hands up slowly along my chest.

Bingo.

Her hands linger there and those stunning, green eyes, with sparkling flecks of gold, find mine.

Desire.

No more waiting.

My lips frantically find hers and they take. They take what they've wanted for weeks now. My tongue dances eagerly with hers and our kiss becomes rushed and uninhibited. She pushes my jacket off my shoulders as I reach for the ties on her robe, pulling at the bow, leaving her toned but delicate body exposed in the absolute best kind of way. Just as my hands glide down her flawless, ivory skin towards her panties, I hear a slight whimper.

"Wait." She steps back, grabbing her robe and covering herself, walking toward the door. "No. We can't do this."

"Sarah?" It comes out as a question. "What is it?"

Her back is to me now, which makes gauging her reaction

tough. She quickly wraps herself back up in her robe, safe, no longer exposed and vulnerable.

"That was a mistake. You...you need to leave. I can't do this with you."

"Sarah, tell me what's wrong." I give her a few seconds to answer. "Who hurt you?"

"My past isn't any of your business. I need you to leave, please." Her soft eyes harden and fill with anger, and a hint of fear.

"Look," I say as I turn her to face me, rubbing my hands up and down her arms. "That kiss wasn't one-sided, love. You gave as good as you got. You were every bit as into it as I was. You can't fake that. And just to be clear, I am *not* the guy who hurt you in the past. I'm the one who wants to be with you right now, right in this moment. Can't you give that a chance?"

"Who told you about him?" She backs away, out of my reach, pulling her robe tighter around her body. One single tear falls from her eyes. I feel helpless when I reach to wipe it away, only to see her flinch when I do. With the sleeve of her robe, she takes care of that tear herself. Only the stain of it remains.

"No one told me anything, Sarah. No one had to. It's written all over your face, and I see it in the way you act towards men in general, not just me. You've completely closed yourself off."

"Then that's my problem, not yours."

"Oh, sweetheart, it is indeed my problem. You see, if that kiss didn't do a good enough job explaining it, let me make it clear to you right now. I want you. In no uncertain terms, I want you, badly. I enjoy being with you, hearing you laugh, watching you smile. Everything. We are so much more than friends and you know it."

"I'll only hurt you, Liam. I don't do relationships because

they're too much trouble. They're messy, and when they're over, I'm the one who will be left to wipe up all the shit that's spilled over to dump in the trash. I do sex. That's it."

"Okay. Then we'll just have sex. Nothing more. Friends with benefits." I attempt a chuckle. "It's apparently all the rage these days."

Jesus. What the hell am I thinking here? I know I can't do *just* sex with her. This could completely ruin the friendship we've built so far.

"Liam, please just go. That's really not what you want, and I don't want to muddy the waters any more than we muddied them tonight. Just forget that kiss ever happened." Her mind is made up as she grabs my jacket and walks toward the door, opening it, allowing the cold winds to filter in.

"Not likely, sweetheart. That was, hands down, the most intoxicating kiss I've ever shared with anyone before, and I want more," I say to her as I tuck a few stray strands of hair behind her ear. Leaning in, I kiss her cheek as I take my jacket from her hands. My breath whispers over her skin. "Just so you know I'm a man who gets what he wants. And I want you."

The front porch squeaks just a little as I hop down from the edge, landing in the grass near my car. Once inside, I glance up to see her standing at the door, her hand on her cheek where I just kissed her.

This isn't over by a long shot, baby.

Chapter Four

SARAH

"Bye, Miss Witten! See ya tomorrow!" little Alyssa yells as she heads toward her bus, blissfully unaware that tomorrow is Saturday.

"Monday, Alyssa. See you Monday, sweetheart!" I call out to her.

"M'kay Miss Witten! See ya tomorrow!" I laugh, thinking how much most of these little kids love school. Hand to God, I think some of these kids would come to school on Saturdays if we'd let them.

Thankfully, she's the last one in the class to leave, which leaves me alone for a few minutes to catch my breath. Some days, most days, seven-year-olds have too much energy. I am exhausted and ready to go home and relax. My eyes are closed as I sit in my chair for a moment's peace. I have my bottle of wine in the fridge and about eight chapters to finish in my book. That's the extent of my agenda for tonight. Just me, wine, and romance...in a book, that is.

That thought has my mind circling back around to Liam, again. He has consumed my thoughts ever since he left my house six nights ago. He's gone silent, though, and I don't know what to make of that. He was so adamant that he wanted to be with me, that there was something between us. And God help me, I know there is, but I can't let my heart go there, especially not with Liam.

So, I watched the man who I knew would completely rock my world, and leave me with the most earth-shattering orgasm ever, walk out my door. The man who would play my body like the guitar he strums so rhythmically onstage at Sam's. The man who is too dangerous for my heart. Too smooth. Too charismatic.

It's totally not fair to think, and completely unreasonable to expect, but I guess I just assumed he'd be around more. I even went to Sam's last night with Raina because Zane was tending bar, but he was nowhere to be found. Cole found us, then found his harem of bimbos that followed him around like some lost puppy. However, much to my dismay, no Liam.

I walk from the school to my car, my mind still reeling over the events of this past week. Starting up my clunker of a car is always a crapshoot, but it revs up just fine this afternoon and I take off toward home. As usual, the ride is uneventful, and I'm thankful I don't live too far from the school so the commute isn't a long one. Just as I pull into the driveway, my cell phone buzzes. It's Raina.

Shit. I forgot to wait for her.

"Hey, chick!" she shrieks. "You left school without me, and you were supposed to give me a ride. Were you even listening to me at lunch today?"

So, my mind's been on other...things right now. Things that are turning me into some kind of hot mess. Getting my shit together is way easier said than done.

"God, I'm sorry. I'm turning around right now. On my way!"

I click the end call button on my steering wheel and make my way back to school. Raina is waiting there, teacher totes in hand, when I arrive. Pulling up next to the curb, I ready myself for the tongue-lashing I know I deserve. I'd like to say *if looks could kill*, but she looks more amused than anything. Some days, I think she's too damn happy.

The door opens and in bounces my best friend. She seriously bounces.

"You look as happy as a loon standing there. Why do you always have to smile?"

"Smiling's my favorite!" she screams, eyes wide, mimicking the character from our favorite Christmas movie. Both of us laugh as I pull the car away from the school and onto the road home.

"My car is still in the shop, babe, so can you pick me up and go with me to Sam's tonight? Zane has to tend bar again. I wish they'd hire someone soon because all the nights away from each other are starting to wear on me a bit."

I feel like a *poor you, boo-hoo* reply is totally in order, but then she'd go in for the kill. I'd hear all about how wonderful life is with a man around. Sex on the regular, cuddling on cold winter nights, and all the romantic, lovey-dovey crap I don't need to hear right now. Then she'd start on how I need to make room in my life for Liam, like she did with Zane. How she gave him a chance and they found their happy ever after, so I should find mine, too. It's like she shits rainbows and farts glitter. I love her, don't get me wrong. I just don't need to be reminded daily of what people think my life is missing without a man.

"I've got a bottle of wine with my name on it, sweets, but I'll take you over and drop you off, if that's okay?"

"Liam and Cole are playing tonight," she replies in a sing-song voice, like the first graders she teaches.

"Goodie for Liam and Cole. I'm sure Cole's brood of bimbos will be hanging around, so maybe they'll both get lucky." Even as these words leave my mouth, I can feel my stomach tighten with anger thinking of him with someone else. What in the ever-loving-hell is happening to me?

I need to keep driving, get Raina home so she can get ready to go out, and keep my mouth shut.

AFTER A FEW HOURS at home to grab a bite to eat and a warm bath, I'm out the door again. I pick up Raina, only a few minutes late, and we head to Sam's. There's an empty parking space available, which is unusual for a Friday night, so I pull up to the bar, leaving the car running.

"You need to come in for a drink, babe. Pleeeeaaase?"

"What the hell, Raina? Are you, like, ten?"

"Just one drink, then you can go home. You can even have water if you want."

I'm trying to toss Raina out the door, but she's digging her heels in and won't get the hell out. God, why do I put up with her?

"If I go in for one drink, will you promise me you'll stop this *you really need a man* bullshit? It ain't happening."

"Hmmm...perhaps." I'd like to silly-slap that smile right off her gorgeous face, but I laugh instead.

Honestly, I don't know why I bother trying to fight her on this. She won't let it go, and most likely, she'd text me the rest of the night with the play-by-play of Liam and Cole's antics. And that shit I do *not* need to hear.

"One drink, then I'm going home. I have toilets to clean and laundry to do and dust to wipe."

Raina just laughs, and I know that evil laugh is the one that means she is *so* not going to let this Liam and me thing drop.

We enter the pub together, and I'm quickly reminded of the real reason I didn't want to come here tonight. Because

24

there is Liam, all sexy with his boots, ripped jeans, and a black tee that fits him like a damn glove. His smile becomes wider as he settles his eyes on me, raising his eyebrows in surprise.

Damn it.

Raina nearly stumbles as I reach for her arm, pulling her quickly to the bar for a seat as far away from the stage as I can possibly get. Only, too bad for me that every single damn seat in this place is visible from the stage, and when I quickly glance at said stage, Liam is chuckling, and shaking his head as he plucks his guitar with firm, smooth movements. All of a sudden, my eyes zero in on those fingers and my mind races with all the things they could do, causing me to wiggle around on my barstool uncomfortably at the thought.

One drink. I can do this. One drink, then I can get home and away from this temptation. No man is worth the kind of heartache I've endured in the past. I won't let him in. I can't. All because of Daniel.

Daniel.

Will I ever be able to put all that to rest? He is precisely the reason why I rarely go back home to visit family. Watching him with my sister and their little girl is too much. To this day, neither of them know I had just learned I was pregnant when I walked in on him with my sister. Granted, the pregnancy was an accident, and I wasn't ready to be a mother that young because I could barely take care of myself. Yet, the baby was real, the baby was Daniel's, but Daniel was no longer mine. He belonged to my sister then and still does today.

My mind continues to drift off to places I don't want it to go.

Miscarriage.

"Your baby's gone, sweetie."

"You'll be fine, sweetie."

"It was just meant to be this way, sweetie."

Fuck.

For the record, I didn't mean to order a second drink, or a third, or a fourth. It just felt too good to keep drinking and too good to stop remembering.

Liam and Cole keep playing, and one song leads to another. One drink leads to another, and before I know it, I've had way too much.

In the far distance, I can still hear Liam's melodic voice singing a David Nail cover tune.

Chapter Five

LIAM

Watching Sarah put away drink after drink is making me very nervous, and because I'm playing, there's nothing I can do. There is something troubling her, and I know it's not just what happened between the two of us days ago. She drifts off occasionally, to a place where it seems she doesn't want to be. Her darkened eyes squint, her forehead wrinkles, and she shakes her head, as if trying to banish the unpleasant thoughts from her mind. She's angry.

I'm angry too, but certainly not at her. Coping with hurt is different for different people, but it's obvious she's not coping at all. She's struggling.

Once our final set is finished, I ask Cole to tear down the equipment as I slide my guitar into its case. This old, blue acoustic has been mine for over twelve years, so I take very good care of it. My father taught me to play on this guitar and I treasure each of those moments with him. My family is still very close, but I don't see them as often as I'd like.

"Damn, man. I always clean up. I've got two blondes waiting for me." He points them out to me, and all I can do is shake my head. He's got a different woman every night he's here. "You should take one off my hands. Wouldn't be a hard-ship, you know."

"Not on your life. They'll have to wait...for just you. I want no parts of that. And for the record, I cleaned up the last two times we played."

"Shit," he grumbles, as he turns to unplug amps and roll up cords. I hop off the stage and head to the bar where I see Sarah on the barstool giggling, snorting almost, at something funny Raina just said to her. She nearly falls out of her seat, but I catch her just in time before she tumbles.

"Whoa...Sarah, you okay?"

"Oh my God, Liam!" She turns unsteadily toward me. Her beautiful eyes look empty, drunk. "Your singing is soooo good. Your voice sounds like an angel."

Jesus. She's just about shitfaced.

"Babe, what have you been drinking?" I'm trying my best to get her situated in her seat when Raina comes back from the restroom.

"How much did she drink, Raina?"

"She's fine. She needs to let loose a little. She's only had a few."

"Oh, shoo," Sarah chirps, waving her hand in my direc-tion. "Just had one drink. Definitely not Jack and Coke. It's burns. Did you know Jack and Coke burns when it goes down, Liam? Okay, two. I promise I only came in for one because you just do that to me. You make me need just one drink so then I can leave, and I don't have to see you, and so I don't have to feel anymore."

So I don't have to feel anymore.

She delivers that line with such sadness in her eyes that it rips me right in two. She absolutely feels something for me. I knew it that night at her house when I kissed her. A woman does not kiss with that much passion if she doesn't feel something. I should totally leave her alone, leave her with Raina. Let her work through all her shit on her own and keep my face out of her business. That would be the smart thing to do.

I've never been the smart one of the family, though, and therein lies the problem.

I take Sarah's hand and whisper to Raina that I'm taking her home. The smile that lights up Raina's face makes me laugh. She's been trying to push Sarah and me together almost from the time we met. To be honest, when I first met Raina and Sarah, my initial reaction was a bit more, shall we say, visceral to Sarah. Her eyes, however, told me she was completely unavailable. That was my cue to stay away. So, I had drinks with Raina, but I knew immediately we'd only ever be friends. I recognized very early on how she looked at Zane.

"Let's go, sweetheart. Let's get you home."

"Liam, *sweetheart,*" she says, mimicking my voice. "I'm not going anywhere with you. Because I know what will happen. You'll make me like you more than I already do. You'll make me fall in love with you and you'll break my heart. Because they all do, you know."

And there's the dagger to my *heart.*

"Let me help you get home. I promise I'll leave as soon as you get in the door." The funny thing about that statement is I actually believe I'll keep that promise. I'm not entirely sure who I'm trying to kid here.

"You promise?" she asks, walking alongside me on unsteady legs, holding on to me like I'm her savior, as we make our way to the front entrance. I refuse to answer and she doesn't ask again.

The coolness of the night air blows in as I open the door, the light of the moon brightening up the sidewalk. My arm instinctively goes around her, pulling her close to keep her warm when she shivers. If only she would let me in, let me take care of her like I am right now. I can be that guy for her, I'm certain.

"My car is right up here. Can you make it?"

"I'm fine." A curt reply.

Now, I know I'm a man, and there are a shit ton of things I do *not* know about women, even with two sisters, but what I do know is when a woman says she's *fine*, what she's really saying is...well, I don't know what she's really saying. All I know is that she is not, in fact, fine.

"Okay. Let me get the door for you." I have no idea how to even reply to the "I'm fine" statement, but at least I can be a gentleman.

Once I get around to my side of the car, I hesitate for just a moment, take a deep breath, and then slide into the driver's seat. I have to do a double take when I glance in Sarah's direction and see that she is out. Like a light. Her piercing green eyes are closed, that beautiful face isn't twisted up in frustration, and for the first time in weeks, she looks utterly relaxed. I can't stop myself as I reach out, caressing her porcelain skin. My thumb draws circles around her cheek and I almost lose it when she leans into my hand, snuggling in for warmth and comfort.

"Baby, you are going to be the death of me," I whisper. "You better be ready, because this time, I'm making you mine." I lean across the console and kiss her forehead, leaving my lips there for a second longer than I should.

"Liam?" It's a whimper from her luscious lips.

"Yeah, baby?"

"Please don't hurt me," she whispers in a very sleepy voice.

"Never. Never in a million years."

Chapter Six

SARAH

My head. Jesus, my head aches.

I turn slowly in my bed and reach for the drink I always put on my nightstand before I go to sleep. It's not there. Why isn't there a drink on my stand?

Holy cannoli! My head is ready to explode.

Oh, God. Last night.

"Jeez. What the hell did I drink?" I say to myself.

"It wasn't Jack and Coke. At least that's what you told me."

I spin around too quickly, nearly tumbling out of bed. Oh, shit. Liam.

"Whoa there. Careful, babe."

Why the hell is he in my bedroom, sitting in my over-stuffed reading chair? I grab for the sheets and the blanket, covering myself as quickly as possible. I need to slow way the hell down because my head is spinning from moving too fast. After a few seconds, I'm able to sit up and ask him what the hell he's doing in my bedroom, in my chair.

"Well, once I managed to get you into the house, I thought it best to put you in your bed where you'd be more comfortable." Why is he smirking?

"Then why are you still here?" *Looking sexy and hot like you always do.*

"You were drunk. There was no way I was leaving you by yourself in that condition. And if I recall correctly, you asked me, several times, in fact, if I would crawl into bed with you and 'snuggle.'"

"Snuggle? You are so full of shit. There's no way I said *snuggle*. I don't even like snuggling." I turn away, obstinately crossing my arms and letting out a huff. Snuggling is excessively personal and way too, I don't know, romantic or intimate or some shit. So, no to the snuggling.

"Suit yourself. I'm just repeating what you asked. Anyway, I need to get going." He rises from the chair and stretches his arms into the air, his shirt slipping out of his jeans that sit low on his perfect hips, showing me a glimpse of his defined abs, and that happy trail all women know leads to paradise. "I just wanted to be sure you were okay when you woke up. And just so you know, I slept here in the chair and not in your bed. So, no snuggling last night."

He casually walks closer to my side of the bed, putting both hands on either side of my body, dipping the mattress slightly and leaning in close. "Sweetheart, when I'm finally in this bed beside you, it won't be to snuggle. There are so many more exciting things to do here, don't you think?"

I can't breathe. Literally, I think I've forgotten how to breathe. It's in then out, right?

He retreats slightly and uses his hand to tuck a few stray hairs behind my ear. The one he just whispered into. The whispering that sounded just like sex. Slow, sensual sex. Lazy sex with Liam.

I think he hypnotized me. He's a fucking hypnotist, I know it.

"I'm heading out. I'll be back to pick you up for dinner around six. I'll see you then, beautiful." And just like that, he's walking out of my room.

Why am I still sitting here? Who the hell does he think he is? How is it that I'm wearing just my panties and a T-shirt? Did he take my clothes off last night?

"Wait. No." Scrambling out of bed, I run toward the door. "I'm not going on a date with you Liam. I told you the other night–"

"Yes, you are," he promptly turns and interrupts.

"Wait...what?" Liam is not a bossy person, so where the hell did this come from? And why do I find it hot?

"You *are* going to dinner with me. End of. It's just dinner, not a date. You have to eat, right? So, you'll eat with me," he says so casually, smiling like an idiot.

I lift my chin in an act of defiance and cross my arms, almost furious. "You can't just demand that I go eat with you, Liam. That's not how it works." Within two, maybe three seconds tops, my arms fall to my sides, and I take a few steps back as he saunters toward me in that lazy, sexy way he does. I need to look away, but I'm frozen.

This isn't me. I don't just follow orders when a man belts them out. They listen to me and do what I say. *That's* how it works.

He threads his fingers through my hair at the nape of my neck ever so gently, forcing me to look up at him, and so help me I can't *not* look. And the breathing thing? I'm having a hard time with that again.

"It's dinner. I'll be back at six and you'll be ready. Dress is casual. We're going to the new Italian place." He kisses me on the forehead and the moment I can no longer feel his touch, I miss it. I don't like that. At all.

He opens the door to leave then stops for a moment. He turns his head and his eyes squint, but remain fixed on mine. I've never felt so exposed or vulnerable in my life. He's seeing me. Every fault, every fear, every nuance of my entire being.

Every emotion I think I've ever felt must be on full display right now for him to see.

His eyes relax, and then all he does is simply smile.

And I smile back.

Apparently, I'm going to dinner with Liam at six. We're having Italian. And it's not a date.

Chapter Seven

LIAM

Giving myself a mental pep talk makes me sound like a pussy. A big one, in fact. But I'm readying myself to knock on Sarah's door and take her to dinner. This morning, I decided to take matters into my own hands and explain to her how things were gonna go. The limb I went out on didn't break and I didn't fall flat...thank fuck. She is a feisty woman, no doubt, and I was a bit apprehensive with how that approach was going be perceived. But apparently, there's a tiny bit of submissiveness hiding inside that headstrong personality of hers. Her response to my demands launched me to a completely new level of surprised.

At six o'clock sharp, my hand raps on her door, and I'm unprepared for what I see when said door opens. Jesus, she's stunning. I take my time inspecting every inch of her, from her over-the-knee boots to her black leggings, up to those firm tits covered with a black tight sweater and opened jean jacket. Her hair is piled on top of her head in some messy bun thing that I know for a fact most women spend hours perfecting. A few strands of her soft hair frame her beautiful face while her vibrant green eyes play shy with mine, blinking a few times.

"Hey," is about all I can get out now, nearly tripping over my words.

"Hey, yourself. You ready to go?"

"Um...yes. Absolutely."

I take her hand in mine and usher her to the car, opening the door for her. Chivalry is not dead, as far as I'm concerned. If I didn't open a car door for a lady, my mother would have my nuts in a sling. I know very well Sarah's capable of opening her own door. She doesn't need a man to do it for her, no woman does. But to me, it's a sign of respect and kindness, and her smile tells me she agrees.

Once I'm behind the wheel and pulling out of her driveway, I reach across the console and take her hand in mine, rubbing her wrist with my thumb. I love touching her. The slight hitch in her breath is a good indication she likes it too. I have to chuckle to myself, thinking that if this is all it took, I'd have grabbed her hand and rubbed it a long fucking time ago.

"Is Italian okay with you?"

"This morning, it sounded to me like I didn't have much of a choice, now did it?"

Awfully snarky, but I'll go with it.

"You always have a choice. If you really didn't want to have dinner with me tonight, you wouldn't have been dressed and ready when I got to your house, now would you?"

"Smart-ass," she whispers, just loud enough for me to make out what she said. I laugh, knowing that if I want any chance with this girl, I've got to stay on my game. She is not going to make this easy on me. What she doesn't know, is that I've never backed down from a challenge yet, and I sure as hell won't lose this one. I've never been so captivated by a woman in my life.

The new Italian place is nearly fifteen minutes from her house, and we arrive about five minutes before the reservation time. Taking her hand, we walk into the restaurant, and immediately we're overcome with the scents of garlic and pasta and sauces. It smells heavenly.

"I haven't tried this place yet, but if it tastes as good as it smells, I can hardly wait."

I'd like to point out that there is absolutely nothing sexual about what she just said. However, I need to close my eyes and think of painting, or baseball, or fixing my car, because the visual of smelling and tasting her assaults my mind and I can't go there right now. We're in a restaurant, not her bedroom. See what this woman does to me?

We're seated quickly. Thank God. Because at least now I can concentrate on the wine list and the menu instead of the intoxicating woman sitting across from me.

The waiter offers his recommendations and shares with us the specials for the evening, then walks away, giving us time to make our choices.

"Everything sounds delicious. What do you think you're having?" she asks, again not knowing what that simple question just sounded like in my horny mind.

You.

"Probably lasagna. It's always been a favorite. My mom usually makes it when I go home to visit."

"Then I'll try that too. Do you go home to see your family often?"

The waiter interrupts us, so I take it upon myself to order for us both.

"We'd like the lasagna, Italian dressing on the salads, and a bottle of Cabernet Sauvignon."

"Excellent choice," the waiter replies, taking our menus, and as he leaves, I return my attention to Sarah.

"So, you asked about my family. I have two sisters, and of course, Mom and Dad. The five of us grew up outside of Durham. One sister is older, one is younger. It was like a rose between two thorns," I say jokingly. "I remember growing up thinking how unlucky I was being flanked by two sisters and having no brothers, until I met Cole in middle school. He's been like a brother to me forever. I talk to Mom and Dad often, but we don't get together as much as we used to."

"It must be nice having a close family." Her head drops, and there's a hint of sadness in her voice. I want to ask her to elaborate on that, but I think I need to give it some time. While we've been friends for months now, it's been very casual. She doesn't ask personal questions and has never indicated she wanted to know a whole lot about my life. I've allowed her to keep me at arm's length long enough.

I reach across the table, taking her hand in mine, and look at her beautiful face. There is a vacancy in her eyes, a look that's distant and hollow, like the eyes of a plastic baby doll. No emotion.

Shit.

"Tell me about your teaching. I want to know what it's like managing seven-year-olds all day." She smiles and her expression quickly changes from sorrow to warmth and love. This, this is her passion.

"Oh my God. It's the best. I've always loved working with children, and I knew very early on I wanted to teach. These kids...they're like little sponges. They soak up everything I teach them, and ask for more. It's a good age because generally they haven't been exposed to all the bad things that happen in the world. They just love life. At least, most of them anyway."

Sarah continues to describe her typical days with twenty

second graders with so much enthusiasm and compassion that it's difficult not to be utterly entranced by her excitement. She lives for these kids.

"Shit, Liam. I'm sorry. I'm totally monopolizing this conversation. You just need to tell me to shut up because I could go on and on forever, you know," she says, giggling and waving her hand around in front of her. The most beautiful sunrise imaginable can't compare to watching this magnificent woman talk about her life with her students. Her eyes are wide, her smile is captivating, and her hands gesture, sometimes wildly, as she becomes engrossed in her storytelling. I'm not completely sure she even noticed the waiter bring the bottle of wine and pour our glasses.

"You are so beautiful." Redness creeps from her neck, up past her cheeks and reaches her eyes, making them shine. And that...that right there is truly spellbinding. She's got me. At this moment, she has me in the palm of her hand.

"Those students are so lucky to have someone like you to love them and teach them. The way you are with kids, you'll make a wonderful mother someday, Sarah."

Her smile wanes, her mood morphing from lively to sorrowful in an instant, and I'm nervous about what I just said. She loves kids, so why wouldn't she want some of her own? Jesus, I've fucked this up already, and I don't even know how. This girl is like a puzzle I'm trying to put together, only she's holding critical pieces so the picture is making no sense.

"Sarah? Are you okay?" I ask hesitantly.

"I'm fine. Good." She takes a drink of her wine and quickly follows it with another. And another.

"Hey. Did I say something wrong?"

"No. You didn't. I'm just tired all of a sudden. Probably the wine, you know. Could we get our meals to go?"

Just then, the waiter brings our plates of lasagna, setting the hot dishes on the table.

"Will there be anything else at the moment?" he asks.

"No, we're good. Thank you." I say, hoping I can get her to stay.

The waiter departs and we're left alone, her looking at me and me looking at her...searching for an answer. An answer I know I won't get tonight.

She lifts her fork, swirls around her lasagna, and then she finally takes a bite. Maybe food is the key here because a smile hints at her lips.

"Good?" I ask, attempting to draw her back into conversation.

"Delicious. Maybe the best I've ever had."

Silence.

"I'm sorry, Liam. There's just more..."

I give her a few seconds to elaborate, but nothing. "More what, sweetheart?"

"Never mind. It's okay. Sometimes I wish certain memories were just bad nightmares instead of being real." Her eyes search mine, unsure and nervous.

"I'm a good listener. I have two sisters, so I am highly qualified to assist with problems of the female population."

That draws a laugh and her muscles visibly relax. "Is that right?"

"Without question. Believe me, I've overheard more than my fair share of female conversation growing up. There were some discussions that were off-limits, but with my quiet, ninja-like movements and reflexes, I was privy to gossip and chit-chat that afterwards I actually wished I'd never heard."

Another chuckle and a quick, but forced smile. "I'll be sure to keep that in mind."

"So, we finish the lasagna and wine here, darlin'?"

"Yes. Absolutely."

Thank fuck.

THE PLATES of pasta and bottle of wine are empty. We stick to generic conversation, which means I'm still getting nowhere. Of course, getting her to dinner is a big step, sure, but I want to know her. *All* of her. Not just the trivial, impersonal things. I take her hand again as we leave the restaurant and walk out into the crisp evening air. Opening her door gives me a chance to be close again, so I take the opportunity to delicately kiss her cheek. Her genuine smile returns as I pull away, heading for her house, all the while having this inner dialogue in my head as to what the hell I'll do when I get her there.

Chapter Eight

SARAH

I don't do nervous with men. Yet, here I sit, wondering why my fingers can't keep still and why they're twisting the hem of my sweater. Repeatedly. My knees bounce and I feel uneasiness when I breathe. This is the third piece of gum I pull out of my purse and begin to chew, along with the other two pieces.

"Sweetheart, three pieces of gum won't do a thing to minimize the garlic you just ate." Liam's hand reaches for mine with the intention of calming me down, but that'll never happen when he's touching me...anywhere. "How about you relax and not worry about anything right now. I'm just taking you home."

So, he *isn't* coming in. Maybe he isn't interested anymore. Maybe it was the way I reacted when he talked about me becoming a mom. Like a freak, right? I couldn't help it, though. I try to keep all that shit locked down and not let my emotions get the best of me when people talk about babies and motherhood. Zane's super sperm is going to knock up Raina before long, so I need to prepare myself for that event. She talks about all the sex they have, and I just know one of those little suckers will drill its way right through the latex barrier, and *boom*! She'll be pregnant. It's going to happen sooner rather than later, so I need to get over my past and just deal.

"Um, would you like to come in...for a little...I mean, for a drink...or something?" My conversations skills are clearly lacking here. Probably due to the lack of oxygen in my brain when he gets so close. Yeah. That must be it.

"I would."

That's it? Just, *I would*?

"Okay. So...okay," I say, shaking my head up and down like an idiot. I used to be able to hang out with Liam and not feel like such an oddball. Suddenly, it's like I'm fourteen again and I'm going on my first date to the high school homecoming dance with the cute boy and a mouth full of braces.

Liam pulls his car into my driveway, then gets out and comes around to open my door, which is something Daniel never did for me. I totally can get my own door for sure, but I could also get used to this feeling of being taken care of. It's endearing and sweet.

Then suddenly I remember I don't want to be taken care of. I can take care of myself. So now those two thoughts are battling it out in my head, like Battlebots, and I'm more aggravated with myself for even considering I need a man around to open a stupid door for me.

We walk up onto the porch and I pull out the key, letting us both into the house.

Once inside, I offer him a drink. The offering I so clearly stumbled over in the car a few minutes ago. I pour us both a glass of wine and we make our way over to the sofa. He makes me smile when he plops himself direct center so that no matter where I sit, I'll be close to him. He grins like the Cheshire Cat, knowing I know he did it on purpose.

It's funny he seems so at home here. He's comfortable in my space and, oddly enough, I quite like that. He holds his glass in one hand, resting his other arm on the back of the sofa. I choose my side and pull both legs up underneath me.

"So, the minor glitch at dinner. What's up?"

"You're direct."

"You have no idea. Tell me."

"I don't think that's really any of your business. We're not dating, let alone exclusively."

"We will be soon enough. What happened at dinner?"

Jesus, he's a demanding somebody. This is territory I'm not ready to enter with him. First of all, the crap with Daniel and my sister is very difficult for me to talk about, but mostly, what will he think of me getting pregnant as a teenager? That I'm irresponsible or that I was some slut trying to trap Daniel into marriage? The only option I have right now is to leave out the pregnancy part. Technically, it's not a lie to not tell the whole story, right?

"It's a long story, and it was a long time ago." I try pulling off an *it-wasn't-a-big-deal* vibe, but he's not buying it. Not sure what made me think he would. He's too perceptive.

"Clearly still affects you, babe, so you can tell me."

A deep breath is the only thing, besides the wine, that calms me at the moment. I look over at Liam and he sits so still, so attentive. For the first time in a long time, I feel like someone, beside Raina, is truly interested in what I have to say. Interested in me. Waiting for me, with no other motive than to just listen.

Here goes nothing.

"I dated a guy, Daniel, my senior year of high school. I'd always had a crush on him growing up. He lived at the other end of my neighborhood. We didn't really grow up together, but I'd known him for a long time, so when he finally asked me out, I was so excited, you know? My sister is a few years older than me, and she kept begging me not to date him. She said he had a reputation and I shouldn't get involved with him."

Before I move further into this story, a newsflash–she was a liar.

"Fast forward to end of senior year, a week after prom. I was out shopping and picked up a Duke sweatshirt for Daniel. That's where he was going to school that fall. I got home early. Too early. Daniel was in my bed..." A lone tear makes its way down my cheek. Before I can brush it away, Liam reaches over, and wipes it away with his thumb. He takes my glass, putting it on the coffee table with his, and pulls me close to him, surrounding me with strength.

"Sweetheart, you don't have to finish. I'm so sorry."

"No. I need to get this out. You wanted to hear it, so just listen." Okay, so maybe a little part of me is demanding too.

"He was in bed with my sister." My heart is nearly in my throat as I speak those few words.

Another tear falls.

And another.

And another.

Each one is brushed away with a gentle swipe to my cheek. Brushed away as if he were not allowing tears for another man to fall in front of him. Brushed away as if he were ridding me entirely of the past and Daniel's betrayal.

Liam's body radiates a strong physical presence and when I lean into him, I fall apart, knowing he will be there to catch me when I do.

He takes his strong fingers and weaves them through my hair, kissing the top of my head. "That never should have happened to you. But I can tell you this." He tugs gently at my hair, causing me to look directly at him. His eyes are narrowed and rigid, the customary softness gone. "That shit says more about Daniel and your sister, and the kind of

45

people they are, than it will *ever* say about you. No one deserves that. Least of all, someone like you."

"Like me? Me, as in breakable? Or foolish?" I snap.

"Absolutely not. You, like in kind-hearted and loving and thoughtful...and beautiful."

"There are some men out there who would completely disagree with that statement."

Liam rolls his eyes and cocks his head to the side. "Can we *not* talk about other men you've been with while you're in my arms?"

"I'm sorry. I didn't mean..."

"I know. And just so *you* know, I'm not those other men, Sarah. This is not a one-off for me, so please don't pretend that it is for you either. Don't lie to me and don't lie to yourself." Liam pulls me so I'm sitting on his lap now, and I get the feeling he isn't done with the inquisition. There's a seriousness to his eyes and his tone. "I know there's more, but I think you've shared enough for now, so I won't pry any further. One day, sweetheart, you'll tell me the whole story."

Did I say he was perceptive? I think I meant psychic. He's a psychic *and* a hypnotist. My stomach churns at the thought of him hearing the whole story. In no way is he going to understand what I went through. That little ending from the *whole story* will go with me to my grave.

Sitting on Liam's lap, being encased in his arms, is so relaxing. This isn't what I'm used to, but I'll admit it feels wonderful. We sit a while in silence, so much so that I nearly fall asleep as the tips of his fingers gently caress my arm. His body shakes slightly with laughter when all I can do is moan.

Soon I feel him shifting, reaching around and lightly smacking me on the ass, catching me completely by surprise. "Now, up you get," he says as he stands, allowing my feet to hit the floor. He holds on to me for a moment until I'm steady.

"I'm gonna head out. I'll see you tomorrow. Cole and I play at the pub, so I'll pick you up around eight."

"You're not staying? I have more wine, if that helps."

"Gotta go, babe." He begins putting on his jacket and I kind of panic. I don't want him to go, but I'm not sure exactly how to get him to stay. So, I go for the usual...it always works.

"But, I thought...you know, I could show you the bedroom?" I say, running my finger up and down his chest. His firm, hard, sexy chest.

Liam grabs my finger, kissing the tip. "I know exactly what you thought, and I'll say it again. I'm not like the other men you've been with. I won't be." He leans in, brushing the stray hair from my eyes, making my skin nearly burn where his fingers touched me. "Here's what's gonna happen. We're gonna see where this attraction leads. We're more than friends, darlin', so you need to catch up. I'm not here for a one-night stand, nor am I interested in a friends-with-bene-fits arrangement." His lips kiss my forehead and my eyes lazily drift shut at the gentleness of it. "I will see you tomorrow at eight."

"Eight. Yeah." That's all I can manage to get out. The scent of his sandalwood cologne and the firmness of his voice have me under some kind of spell. What the hell is he doing to me?

Chapter Nine

LIAM

Cole and I sit in his living room, preparing to get a little practice in before tonight. We've got a few new songs to add to the set list, and we need to rehearse the music and the lyrics. Unfortunately, the only thing on my mind is Sarah. I've thought of nothing else since I left her last night, and believe me when I say I did *not* want to leave. She offered to *show me her bedroom*–code for let's have sex–and if I thought we were never going to be more than friends, I'd have totally taken her up on that. I was rock hard by the time I got to the car, and the monster was ready to come out and play. It's hard, literally, not thinking with my dick because, full disclosure here, that's what I did for years as a teenager. I won't be that guy with Sarah. She means too much.

"Earth to Liam. Man, what the hell? Where's your head today?" His voice seems distant because my mind is obviously on my hot little brunette.

"Sorry, man. I'm good. Let's get on this."

"You're not good. You're out in left fucking field. You need to just bang her and get it over with."

Red. That's all I see.

"What the hell, Cole? Are you serious right now?" I can't believe he said that. I'm up out of my seat, running my hands through my hair so I don't grab him by the collar and shake the shit out of him. "You're talking about Sarah, not some random groupie you decide to drag home for a quick roll. Show some respect."

"Jesus. I'm sorry, man." Both hands go in the air as if to surrender. "You're really into her, aren't you?"

"Yes. And I'm having a hard time making her believe I'm not like every other asshole she's been with. I won't be a one-and-done with her," I reply, pacing back and forth. "Plus, the shit she shared with me last night is gonna make it even harder to get through to her."

"Wow. It's just, you two have been hanging out like best friends. I didn't realize. Should have said something."

"S'all good, man. She's just different, you know."

"Okay, then. So, no *just banging*. You're a good man, bro, so I hope she knows what a catch you are," he huffs.

After a few moments of silence, Cole breaks it in typical Cole fashion.

"Well, are we gonna sit around braiding each other's fuckin' hair and doin' nails, or are we gonna practice?"

"Fuck you, man," I say, laughing. "Let's get it then."

OUR PRACTICE SESSION lasts until well after lunchtime. We've got these new songs nailed down and we're ready for tonight. My sister called early this morning to let me know she and her new man are coming to hear us play. I'm excited about that since Sarah will get to finally meet some of my family. Add to that, the new boyfriend is also a musician and his old man is part owner of a recording label.

After Cole and I bought into Sam's with Zane, I was content to run the finances of the bar and play music with Cole when we could. The business degree I had earned would help me with my new role as part-owner, and with the new business we've been getting, and the improvements we're making to the pub, I figured I'd settle here and make a life.

Mom and Dad always encouraged my sisters and me to live the life we wanted and do what we loved to do. They were both musicians, as Dad taught music at NC State and Mom coordinated the choral program at the high school I attended. I have music in my blood, I guess you could say. There are many fond memories of the five of us sitting around the backyard fire pit on comfortable fall evenings and listening to Dad strum the acoustic while Mom sang her sweet tunes.

Now, knowing some of our performance tonight could possibly end up being put in the hands of a record exec, I'm not certain about anything. Throw Sarah into the mix and I feel as confused as hell. Mom always told me things tend to work out for the best, so I'm going to go with the flow and see what happens. No sense in borrowing trouble.

SARAH ISN'T QUITE ready to go when I get to her place at eight, although she could wear baggie sweats and a tee and look beautiful. Hearing her cuss and rant about her hair in the bathroom makes me laugh.

"What's so funny?" And there she stands, hands on hips, tapping the toe, mad as a pissed off hornet.

"Babe, you look fine."

Oh shit. I said it. Here it comes.

"Just fine? Fine isn't good enough, Liam, if I'm meeting your sister tonight. Fine isn't good enough."

She's still standing there, on the brink of tears, when I reach for her and pull her close. I place both my hands on her pink cheeks, tipping her head back and planting a kiss on her lips that will make her forget she even has hair. Her hands come to my biceps and she squeezes as her tongue swirls around, twirling and battling with mine. Kissing her like this can literally bring me to my knees. Her hips are in close proximity to my dick when she goes up on the tips of her toes, and I'm nearly undone.

The kiss ends, not by my choice, and she stares at me, a hint of a smile passes over her lips.

"You messed up my lipstick."

"Better your lipstick than your mascara, babe. Go reapply and let's get going. You're beautiful, so don't make me tell you twice."

"Yes, sir. Whatever you say," she whispers and winks as she turns to walk away.

Holy. Shit.

Not more than two minutes later, she emerges from the bathroom, plump red lips redone, and we're ready to put on coats to head to Sam's.

MY SISTER AND HER MAN, Roman, are walking into the bar just as we get there, so we all walk in together. It's not as busy as a weekend night, but the crowd is still somewhat noisy.

"Sarah, this is Tatum, my sister, and her boyfriend, Roman. Guys, this is Sarah."

"It's so great to finally meet you. Liam talks a lot about

you," my sister says, smiling and leaning over for a hug. No handshakes here.

"Is that right?" she asks, smiling at me, grabbing my elbow. "Well, Liam and I have been friends for a while. I'm glad to meet you both, and I'll be anxious to hear some funny baby Liam stories while you're here."

Tatum pipes up, "Oh, there are plenty," and both girls giggle at my expense.

"Roman, let's get drinks at the bar."

"Good idea," he says, rolling his eyes at the two grown women who cackle like teenagers.

We head over to get our drinks where the new bartender, Samantha, takes our orders.

"Thanks for bringing Tatum tonight. The drive wasn't too bad, was it?"

"Nah. Not at all. I'm going to get a couple videos on my phone to send to Dad, if that's okay. Tatum says y'alls song-writing is amazing."

"Been writing songs for years. I love it."

"Sweet. I'm excited to hear them." Roman looks over to where the girls are sitting, and we both shake our heads, laughing. "We should get back to the women, because God knows what stories they're swapping right now."

"You got that right."

Samantha hands us our drinks, and we head back over to where the girls are sitting side by side. Sarah and Tatum are getting along perfectly, just as I knew they would. Tatum has such an outgoing personality and makes friends so easily. Since Sarah is a bit on the extroverted side as well, I had a feeling they would hit it off.

Sarah stands when we return, knowing I need to get to the stage for tonight's gig. The pink in her cheeks darkens when she blushes after the heated kiss and the smack on the ass she gets before I leave.

"I'm headed up to the stage. Enjoy the music, guys."

"Break a leg, Liam!" my sister pipes in.

With that, I meet up with Cole and we finish setting up amps and mics and guitars. In no time, we're ready to go.

෧෧

OUR FIRST SET sounds even better than this morning's practice session, and I can tell Roman is impressed. He looks at Tatum often and smiles. He's used his phone to record some of our performance, and I'd love to know when that recording will land in the hands of his father. My mind has conjured up all sorts of scenarios. All the way from *you're good, but won't make it in the industry* to *you're going to be music legends and superstars*. But let's face it, I'm inclined to believe the former since the music business is a tough nut to crack.

I make my way back to the table after our first set and wiggle my way into a spot beside Sarah. Leaning in, I kiss her neck and whisper, "I'm so happy you're getting along with my sister and Roman. I can tell she likes you, and that's important to me."

"She and Roman are great. They're so cute together too," she says, hunching her shoulders and wrinkling her nose. "He looks at her like she hangs the moon."

"Kinda like how I look at you then?" The compliment throws her a bit, and she squirms nervously in her seat, keeping her eyes from finding mine. I'll let that go for now. "So, what'd you all think?"

Roman is the first to offer his opinion. "Liam, you and Cole sound amazing. The way your voices harmonize is fantastic. So in tune with each other. Best sounding duo I've heard, man," he offers, holding out his hand for a handshake.

"Nice. Thanks for that."

"Not blowing smoke, man. You sound perfect. Do you do

any originals?" he asks, finishing off his beer, and then motioning to the server to bring us another round.

"We absolutely have some originals, but we don't do too much of that here, though. Mostly people like to listen to covers of their favorites."

"Would you mind doing one? I'd love to shoot one off to Pops, if that's cool with you."

"Absolutely. We'll rearrange the next set a bit and fit one in."

"Gah! I can't wait. I'm sure your dad will love them," Tatum says, clapping her hands and bouncing excitedly.

Sarah looks at Roman, then back to me, confused. I decide to keep the fact that Roman's dad is a record exec to myself for now. The old *I know someone who knows someone who knows someone in the business* usually doesn't pan out, so no sense in getting her upset about any of this right now.

Just then, Raina and Zane head our way. Sarah stands for a hug, then pulls her down to the seat and introduces her to Tatum. Zane takes a seat next to Roman who moves closer to Tatum.

"Tate, babe, my lap is wide open." Roman gestures as she moves damn near right on top of him to make room for everyone.

"No need, sis. I've gotta scoot back up to the stage." I love my sister, but I do *not* need to see her giving her man a lap dance in the middle of my bar. Eyebrows raised, it's apparent that fell on deaf ears since I see not only Tatum plopping down on Roman, but Raina has found Zane's lap to be wide open as well. Sarah and I just look at each other in amusement.

"Maybe I can get a lap dance later, babe."

And she shoos me off, laughing the whole time.

❦

COLE and I are in the zone tonight. There's dancing, singing along, and lots of applause when we finish for the night. By far, it's the best we've sounded and we both feel relatively positive about what Roman will send to his dad.

"Bro, it was great to see you. You sounded amazing, as usual," Tatum announces before she and Roman head out.

"Give Mom and Dad hugs from me when you get back. I need to visit real soon," I say as I walk them to the entrance of the pub, giving my sis a big hug. I'm so lucky to have family like I do. "Drive safe." Tatum and Roman take off, headed back to Durham.

It's sad that Sarah doesn't have that same kind of relationship with her sister. Tatum acts like more of a sister to Sarah than her own. Maybe that kind of relationship is something she's been missing, so I hope that meeting Tatum, and getting along so well will help her.

Samantha and Zane have just about everything cleaned and ready to shut down for the night behind the bar, as Cole, Raina, and the rest of the servers work on the tables and sweeping the floors.

Everyone says goodnight and we all leave the bar together. Just as Sarah and I reach my car, I pull her close to me then back her up so she's leaning against the hood. The coolness of the night is quickly overtaken by the heat of the moment.

"Liam?"

"What, baby?" My nose sweeps behind her ear, and Jesus, she smells so good, her scent so sweet and subtle.

"Um...what are you doing?"

"If you need to ask, then I'm doin' it all wrong," I whisper, low and soft. "There's no one around this late, and the streets of this small town are rolled up and put away for the night. I could lay you back on the hood of this car right now."

She giggles. I don't want her giggling. I want her panting

and writhing. I want her beneath me, craving my touch like nothing else she's craved in her life. Remember when I said I was a patient man? My patience is wearing thin.

"You know I absolutely loved tonight. You getting along so well with Tatum." Sarah's coffee-colored hair is soft to the touch and my hands automatically thread their way through those luscious locks. I may never get enough of her.

She swallows hard as I use my tongue to delicately trace the sensitive skin behind her ear.

"Li–Liam, you're just on a high from how well you performed...ummm...tonight. I...mmmm," she sighs, "think you should probably take me home now."

"I'll take you home. But, you need to know, baby, that I want this so much with you. So much it's nearly killing me. And I know you want me too." My hands continue their assault on her body, my lips eagerly finding hers. I feel her breathing accelerate and when I pause to look at her, those green eyes turn dark with need. She says nothing in response, simply smiles shyly and nods.

"Let's go." I take her hand and usher her as quickly as I can into the car.

Chapter Ten

SARAH

My heart is nearly beating out of my chest. Liam has me so wound up it's hard for it to find the right tempo to beat normally. He is dangerous with that easy smile and that gentle touch. He damn near rendered me speechless, which is tough to do because I always have a lot to say. My tongue is altogether twisted at the moment, and I can't seem to find the words to tell him that maybe this is not a good idea. I'm getting too caught up in him, falling too fast for him.

"Stop thinking, Sarah. I told you before, we're seeing where this is going. If you're not ready for me right now, that's okay. I'm not going to push. But this," he says, waggling his finger between us, "is happening. Sooner or later, it's going to happen."

Liam pulls in the driveway, puts the car in park, and before I can make a move, he's leaning across the console with his hand cupping my face, and that subtle touch spreads fire over my skin. He doesn't say a word, just stares, his eyes softening as they find mine. We sit like that for a minute. A minute that quite possibly feels like a lifetime.

"Invite me in, babe. Please, let me in."

"Okay," I whisper softly. That's the only answer there is. *Okay.*

I'm letting my guard down.

I'm letting him in.

I'm scared to death.

And by the look on his face, he knows it.

"Sweetheart, I am *not* Daniel, and I sure as hell am *not* the one-night stands you've had since you broke up with him. If I could, I'd hunt that bastard down right now and kick his ass for what he did to you. But instead of looking *for* him, I'd rather look *at* you while we make love. I'm going to make love to you, and I want to be buried so deep inside of you that the only man's name you'll ever remember is mine."

See what I mean? Dangerous.

I'm sitting in his car, my clothes aren't even off, and for the second time in less than forty-eight hours, I feel exposed and vulnerable. He sees me in a way no one ever has before. My heart says I can trust him. My head tells another story altogether.

My heart. I go with my heart. He is different, I feel it.

"Okay. Okay, Liam," I say, nodding my head up and down. "Please don't make me regret trusting you."

The softness and reassurance I see in his eyes tells me he knows my fear, but that my heart is safe with him. This man knows me.

In the blink of an eye, Liam is around to the passenger side of the car, opening the door, holding out his hand to me. Giving him my hand means I'm giving him my heart. We both know what's going to happen tonight.

Once inside, I turn on the gas fireplace to help warm the house. Liam helps me out of my jacket and takes his off, throwing it across the oversized chair. I watch those hands that so smoothly strum his guitar as they work to slowly remove my clothes. He's going to play my body like he plays his guitar...rhythmically and in perfect tempo. My insides quiver at the thought.

His hands drag my top over my head and my jeans down over my hips. My body lights up with desire. Desire that I never experienced with any other man before. He stands stock-still, with narrowed eyes that take in every inch of me, a seductive smile slowly spreading across his face. His hands grab mine, pulling them out to the side so that every single inch of me is available for his perusal.

"You are exquisite." His voice is low and strong, his eyes heavy with lust. My body tingles in anticipation of what is to come.

He lightly runs his callused fingertips up and down my arms, leaving goose bumps along their path. Quickly, he pulls me into his hard body and in a matter of seconds, his lips are millimeters away from mine. He's holding me perfectly still, not allowing my lips to touch his, and for a brief moment, his warm breath is mixing with mine. In a slow but deliberate motion, he gently covers my mouth with his. Sensually, erotically, our lips connect, my mouth opening to his, my tongue twisting with his, the delayed intimacy causing heat to pool between my legs. There has never been a kiss like this, so emotional, yet so consuming at the same time.

"The light from the fireplace makes the gold flecks in your beautiful green eyes sparkle. Just gorgeous."

I tuck my chin into my neck in an attempt to stop the blush, but when I hear a deep chuckle, I know it was futile.

"Umm...my bedroom is back this way," I say, pointing through the back of the living room and down the hallway. I'm nervous, and he knows it, because he's already been in my bedroom, the night he brought me home when I got trashed at Sam's. But I can't overthink this, or over analyze, or I'll draw a line with Liam that I don't think I want to.

"And this rug in front of the fireplace is right here." He begins removing his clothes piece by piece, and I can't help but stare. I'm not entirely sure I've even blinked my eyes yet. Not that I care, really. His body is statuesque, a work of art. Strong, broad shoulders, the well-defined lines of his chest and abs, the deep, sexy V at the tops of his hips, and his long muscular legs complete this outrageously fit man.

"Jesus," I whisper.

With eyebrows cocked, Liam chuckles and whispers back, "You done, babe?"

Busted.

"Well, you took your time eyeing *me* up, I figured I'd return the compliment. You are one handsome man, Liam Reynolds."

"You are one beautiful woman, Sarah Witten. And now that we've established a mutual respect for each other's bodies," he says, grabbing at my waist and pulling me down to the floor, "let me take some time and worship yours."

He gently lays me down near the fireplace, removing my blue lacy bra and panties, placing kiss after kiss along my shoulders and neck. He leans in for another mind-blowing kiss on my lips, and after a brief stint there, he makes his way down my body, licking, sucking, and driving me out of my mind with need. It's when his tongue lands on my center that I've given up all hope of ever breathing normally again. This man will be the one I measure every intimate encounter against for the remainder of my life. I can tell, already, that no one else will compare. For a moment, I wonder if I even want there to be another man that compares to Liam. I'm falling hard and fast. I feel it.

He takes his time, running his tongue along the bundle of nerves, and within minutes, Liam's swirling tongue has my legs shaking, and my stomach contracting in what is unmistakably the most powerful orgasm I've ever had. My hands claw at the fabric of the rug, my hips bucking up and down uncontrollably. Two firm hands settle on my abdomen in an attempt to keep me still, but fail miserably.

My erratic heartbeat is finally settling as I feel him make his way up my body, his smooth skin grazing mine. Liam's chest rests on mine causing my nipples to harden again with need. Heated flesh on flesh. "God, Sarah. You're magnificent when you come. So beautiful."

His mouth finds mine, his fingers swirl at my wet center, and I'm once again overcome by how skilled Liam is in the art of love-making. I reach my hand down to find his cock, only to have both my hands placed above my head and held there by one of his. His focus is on my pleasure this time, not just him getting off and moving on.

"Please let me touch you."

"Your only job right now is to feel, baby. Just feel," he whispers. "Are you on birth control? Or do I need a condom?"

"I'm on the pill," I whisper, and immediately focus my attention to his body and smile before unwanted memories sweep in.

"I'm clean, Sarah. Please tell me this is okay."

"It's very much okay." How could I not be okay looking at this wonderful, thoughtful man who is about to make love to me.

Warmth envelopes me as a very well-endowed Liam enters me, just the tip at first, rocking into me slowly, carefully, as I become accustomed to his size.

"All good?"

"Oh, God, Liam. Yes."

This physical connection with Liam is so intense that I can feel tears welling up, ready to fall. This isn't just sex for him or for me. There are emotions involved. Serious emotions. Emotions that could break me...again.

The rhythm of his hips picks up to a faster pace, thankfully erasing that thought, then he reaches down, and pulls my leg up, placing it over his shoulder to get deeper inside of me. Faster and faster, he thrusts, sweat breaking out on his forehead. His hand releases mine from over my head, and as soon as he lets them go, they tightly grip his shoulders, holding on and clawing as we both reach our climax together.

His face grimaces as he comes harder than I've ever seen a man come before. My insides are shaking, and my body quivering, quite nearly numb from the onslaught of Liam's punishing thrusts. What has he done to me? What in the ever-loving hell did I just experience?

Liam's body relaxes as it slowly descends to cover mine. He's still inside me as the last small bolts of pleasure rumble through us both. Breaths panting, chests heaving, eyes closed, we still.

No movement.

No words.

No regrets.

Just pleasure.

Liam breaks the silence. "Sarah?"

"Yes?"

"Are you okay?"

"Yes?"

Liam chuckles, right along with me. He rolls off to my side, and I instantly feel the loss, but when he grabs a tissue to clean me, I tense at the intimacy of that. His eyes never leave mine as he wipes away what remains of our pleasure, and what could very well be an embarrassing gesture turns out to be something I've never remotely felt before from a man. I feel cared for, not just used. Soon, Liam is pulling me into him, hiking my leg up over his, and we lay there, completely sated and relaxed.

"I will never get enough of you," I hear him whisper. My mind instinctively goes into protective mode, and I begin to slide out from under him to get away. I have to have some space. This is what I do.

Unfortunately–or fortunately perhaps–Liam isn't having any of it. He tightens his hold around my waist, gripping my hip and lightly smacking my ass, keeping me grounded.

"You stay right here, babe. You're good. We're good. That, darlin', was more than I can find words to describe right now. But, you are *not* going to freak out on me. Just relax."

I do as I'm told, shaking my head and wondering when I started liking my ass smacked, and when I started to consider snuggling as an after-sex activity. As it turns out, I kinda like being taken care of too.

He tosses the tissues aside and soon he has my body folding into his again, feeling his comforting touch and his strength. How has he done this to me so quickly? How has he gotten so far under my skin that I wonder now how I ever managed without him near? This is crazy. But I'm not going to freak out. I'm relaxing. Yes. That's good. I'm relaxed, I think.

"Your mind needs to relax too, babe. Stop thinking. You're messing up my zen."

"Your zen?"

"Yeah. My state of calm. Don't be messin' it up."

And when I twist my head so that I'm looking right into those piercing eyes, I can see humor in them, and the ornery, youthful smile on his face makes me laugh.

"Far be it from me to mess with your zen."

"Damn straight. Now lay here with me and close your eyes," he mumbles, shifting to reach for the blanket on the chair. He settles back in, draping us both with the cover as we lay in front of the fire. Relaxing. Just like he said we should do.

Liam's fingertips gently begin caressing my arm, and all the while, the muscles in my body begin to settle into a state of calm.

I think I'm finding my zen. Who the hell would have ever thought a man would create a calm within me?

After a short amount of time, my eyelids begin blinking much more slowly than normal, deciding to give up the fight and close for good.

Chapter Eleven

LIAM

It's difficult to describe the feeling of finally holding Sarah in my arms. Believe me when I say I wasn't completely sure she'd let me in. I don't think I've ever had to work this hard for a woman in my life. I'd never been what some may call a man-whore. Never slept around for the sake of sleeping around. Knew I wanted to find someone who complemented me, who would just get me and my music and my songwriting. And it's her. It's Sarah.

But damn if she isn't going to be a tough sell. She's convinced herself that all men are dicks and is having such a difficult time really giving me a chance. I mean, I totally get it. She was fucked over in the worst way by that asshole, Daniel, and her bitch of a sister. Jesus, who does that?

Slowly, I move out from under this beautiful woman. She stirs slightly, and then rolls over to her stomach. With the blanket now balled up on the floor beside her, all I see is her sweet, sweet ass. Damn, I can't even look at her without getting hard.

Reaching down, I gently roll her over then slip my arms under her knees and her neck to carry her to bed. Tomorrow is a day off for her, but I need to head over to Sam's for a while to finish some paperwork, so I need some sleep.

Her bed is soft and comfortable and she barely twitches when I curl in beside her. Her back is right up against my chest. And her ass? Well, let's just say I need to think about all the paperwork I have to do, so I don't act on the need to wake her up for round two. My dick and my brain need to be a little more coordinated in their efforts.

I WAKE to the feeling of Sarah trying to extricate herself from my embrace. I chuckle and hold tighter because I will not let her do this. I will not let her regret last night. In the light of day, she's going to try to play this as no big deal. However, I know how big a deal it was to her last night. Her eyes told me everything I needed to know. She didn't need to say a word.

"Where do you think you're goin'?"

"Okay, so, I just need to pee. Seriously. Can I do that or do I need permission?"

Note to self...Sarah's not a morning person...at all.

With the back of my hand, I smack on her ass as she gets up, causing her to yelp as she hustles in to the bathroom. After a few minutes, she comes back out with a robe on. The same one she wore the night I returned her driver's license to her. The one that shows her nipples when they're hard, and that makes us both very, very happy. Both, as in me and little me...well, not so little.

"I've got to go to the bar today and get some paperwork finished. You want to ride along?"

"Oh, so you're asking now?"

I'm out of bed so fast it makes her skittish. My hand grabs at her waist, pulling her to me. "Be careful with that sweet mouth, baby. It could be good for so many things. I'd hate to have to muzzle it," I joke, wiggling my eyebrows up and down.

She finagles out of my hold and makes her way into the kitchen, giggling as she goes. Quickly I get dressed and the sight I see when I hit the kitchen is staggering. Sarah is bent over. All the way over. Oh, she's got on her robe, sure, but I guaran-damn-tee ya she's minus panties.

Wicked, wicked woman.

"Do you want–" She squeals as she turns around, jumping when she sees me there ogling her backside. "You mentioned those ninja skills before, so I guess I shouldn't be surprised I didn't hear you. And what is so good about my ass that you need to stare when I'm bent over?"

"Have you seen your ass?"

"Most women try to avoid looking at their asses, Liam, so include me in that group," she snaps as she turns around to start breakfast.

For the record, I didn't mean to grab her ass quite that hard. Or maybe I did. Either way, she jumps again when I lunge for her and latch on to that fine fanny. Once she's in my arms, I take the opportunity to kiss her slowly, tenderly, all tingles and desire. Kissing Sarah is unlike kissing any other woman. She's all sass and fire, but as soon as my lips make contact with hers, she melts. Her body nearly goes limp and she leans into me so carelessly that I can't help but want more. Much more.

"So, what's for breakfast, babe?"

No response.

"Babe?"

"Oh, um, pancakes?"

I laugh. "Well, you were the one starting breakfast, so I figured you knew what you were going to make. I've got to head out in about a half hour to get to Sam's."

"Then sit," she commands, pointing to the stool with her wooden spoon, which causes me to raise my eyebrows.

"Sit?"

"I mean, please have a seat and the pancakes will be right up. That better?" she sasses.

"Much."

Sarah goes about making pancakes and we sit to share breakfast together. For the first of many, many mornings, I hope. While we eat, she talks about her day off from school and that she and Raina are going to the gym. Since there is rain in the forecast for most of the day, they decide not to run along the Riverwalk but go to the small gym downtown to use the treadmills. And all the while she tells me this, I visualize her in exercise leggings and a sports bra. Remember that ass I mentioned earlier? That ass in leggings stirs up visions of nasty things I'd like to do to this woman.

Once we finish cleaning up, Sarah walks me to the door, grabbing my coat from where I threw it last night. My eyes land on the rug in front of the fireplace and memories come flooding back. I've waited a long time to get this far with Sarah, so now I have to keep the momentum going.

"Dinner tonight. I'll be home around four, so come at five," I request as I make my way down the walkway toward my car.

Sarah stands there, wrapping her robe tighter around her to ward off the chill in the air. "Okay."

"See there. That wasn't so hard, was it?"

Sarah rolls her eyes and lets out a huff. "Goodbye, Liam."

"Goodbye, sweet girl."

Chapter Twelve

LIAM

The knock at the office door of the bar at this time of day is a surprise, and in walks Cole, looking a bit tired and worn down.

"What the hell is wrong with you, man? Some woman stay too long last night?"

"Shit. No woman last night, man. I asked Samantha if she wanted a ride home because I didn't want her walking like she usually does. That worries me, you know. So, I took her home and we just talked most of the night."

"You? Just talked to a woman?"

"Fuck you. Yeah, I did. She's a nice girl. She's nice and...quiet. A little on the pretty side too."

"A little?" It's hard not to laugh at how uncomfortable this is for him. I think he's just a bit smitten with Little Miss Samantha.

"Well, yeah. She is. You know, she's got this hair, and her eyes..."

"Jesus, Cole. Every woman has hair and eyes."

"Shut it, Liam. You know what I mean. She's got pretty hair and pretty eyes."

"Any other words besides *pretty* you can think of?"

"You know what, this convo is over, bro. Anyway, I came to ask if you'd heard anything about the videos from Roman or his old man." Cole takes a seat across from the desk, kicking out both legs and crossing at the ankle while his hands cradle the back of his head, obviously making himself at home while I'm trying to work.

"He just sent the videos last night, so his dad probably hasn't even gotten around to looking at them yet. People like that are busy. He may never see them, so I'm not getting my hopes up. Anyway, he's just one guy. A lot of people would have to like what we do before we'd get any kind of call."

"I know. Hard not to get a little excited, though. Did you say anything to Sarah about it?"

"Nah, man. No sense in even bringing it up until we know something more definite. I've been thinking a lot about what could possibly happen with the bar, though. With the renovations we've done, we're getting busier and busier. I don't think hiring just one new bartender is gonna cut it. We almost need a manager. Someone to take the load off you and Zane and me. We're just too damn busy."

"You got that right. I'll tell you though, Samantha's got a good head on her shoulders. She could manage this place, sure as shit. She took some business classes before. Never got to graduate, but she knows her stuff. I get the feeling she could use the extra money too."

"You seem to know a great deal about our new bartender."

"Shut it. She's nice," he grumps.

"And pretty?" I have to laugh to myself because Cole isn't a one-woman kinda guy. But I'm guessing if it's the right woman, he might be down with that. Perhaps the right woman is named Samantha.

"Damn it, Liam!"

"Teasin'. Settle down. It does sound like we need to meet with Zane then."

"Meet with me about what?" Zane approaches the doorway to the main office.

"About maybe promoting Samantha to manager and hiring another bartender. We're too damn busy, man. We need some help. I talked with her last night for a long time. She'd do a great job. I'm sure of it."

Zane takes a few seconds to calm his laughter. "You? Just *talked* to a woman?"

"What the fuck is wrong with you two? Yeah, we talked." Cole runs both hands through his hair, getting a little more pissed at both of us.

"Zane, Cole said Samantha's taken some business classes. She didn't graduate college or anything, but he seems to think she'd be a good fit."

The three of us grab some drinks and sit around the desk to discuss what responsibilities Samantha would have as a bar manager, and talk about putting out feelers for a new bartender. Once we've ironed all that out, I finish up with the paperwork and make my way to where Zane and Cole are stocking the bar for tonight's crowd. Monday Night Football on our big screen and half-price drafts bring a good deal of business.

"So, you're gonna talk with Samantha, right Cole?"

"Absolutely. I'll keep you posted. And call her Sam. She likes Sam better," he says with the most dumb-ass looking smile on his face.

My eyes find Zane's and between the two of us, I can't tell you who is more confused over this entire conversation about Samantha. I mean, Sam.

"I'll see you guys tomorrow. I'm headed home. Sarah's coming for dinner," I say, as I turn pointing in their direction.

"And before either of you two nitwits say anything, yes, we're finally dating. At least I think so, anyway."

"What the hell does *I think so anyway* mean?" Both those assholes are trying not to laugh.

"It means she's finally softening up to the idea of having a relationship. I just have to work a little harder, that's all."

"Good luck with that, bro!" They apparently love having a laugh at my expense. But I can see the writing on the wall right now. Cole has it bad for our new bartender, soon-to-be bar manager, Sam. He never *just talks* to women. So, he better be ready to get as good as he's giving.

Chapter Thirteen

SARAH

"Seriously though, Sarah. I really think you need to just relax and just go with it. Liam's a good guy. You've been friends with him and hanging out, so you know he's not seeing anyone or even looked at another girl at the bar, and God knows there've been plenty. Cole seems to attract a lot of barflies."

Raina and I have been on the treadmills now for about twenty minutes and she's been relentless the entire time. Problem is, I can't escape.

"I know. I really do. But what happens when this whole thing goes south? Huh? I won't even be able to go to Sam's anymore because he'd be there."

"Who said anything about it going south? Why do you have to doom everything to hell before it even starts? And by the way, how was the sex?"

"How do you know we had sex?" I ask, shooting her a look.

"Ha! I didn't, but you just confirmed it," she all but screams, pointing directly at me.

"Raina, sometimes you act like you're fifteen. And just so

you know, it was amazing." It's hard to keep the smile off my face and the pink from taking over my cheeks.

"Gah!" she shrieks. "I knew it. That man has rhythm, and when a man looks like that *and* has rhythm too? A monster in the sack."

"And you would know this how?"

"Well, I've heard. And maybe read about it in my new romance novel. It's about a rock star, by the way."

"You never cease to amaze me, girl. Look at you, reading all the smut. But oh, God, Raina. It's like he utterly consumes. He's protective and bossy. I don't think I've ever had that kind of experience with anyone else. Definitely not with Daniel. It's just hard to explain the connection that's there. I don't do *connections* but the thought of not being with him? Ugh! How did I let this happen?"

"Some things are just meant to be, babe. I think I remember you telling me that once."

I continue walking in silence, picking up the pace for just a few more minutes, and I mull that statement around in my head. I always thought Daniel and I were meant to be. When I found out I was pregnant, I took it as a sign. Thought for sure that would make our relationship permanent, even though I was only eighteen at the time. So very young.

Shattered is how I ended up when I saw Daniel with my sister, and I was even more devastated when I lost the baby. Growing up, I truly wasn't that close to Sydnee. She was the first-born and mom always seemed to favor her, coddle her, but never in a million years did I ever think she would have done something like that to me. That's a kind of hurt I can't seem to get over. She wanted Daniel all along, which why she tried to talk me out of dating him in the first place. So, what was *meant to be* at that time of my life was losing not only Daniel, but our baby as well.

The treadmill slows down considerably and stops. I hurry

to the small locker room before I break down right here in front of Raina. She would understand this dilemma, sure, but no one else needs to know what a complete idiot I was back then. My mom and I share that secret alone. Dad was so busy with working overtime that he wasn't around too much, and obviously my sister was spending all her time with my boyfriend to even notice there was something wrong.

"I just need to get home," I whisper to no one as I stuff my things into my gym bag.

"What's waiting for you at home?"

"Shit!" I squeal, spinning around to find Raina right behind me. "Why does everyone find it necessary to sneak up on me and scare me half to death? I just need to go. I'm supposed to go to Liam's for dinner, but I'm canceling. I can't do this. I can't do this to him or to me."

Here's where I should know better than to walk out on Raina because it clearly will not end well. It never has. She does not like to be ignored and essentially, that's exactly what I'm doing. No sooner do I turn to leave than she grabs my hand and I stop, hanging my head, not looking at her for fear the tears building up in my eyes will begin to fall.

"Look at me," she insists. "You are not canceling anything. You are going to dinner at Liam's. You are going to leave the shit with Daniel and Sydnee in the past where it belongs. The choice they made was theirs and theirs alone. It's been far too long that they've had this hold over you and you need to stop. Like, now. It's finished and nothing you can do will change a thing that's happened."

"I wouldn't take Daniel back if he were the last man on God's green Earth." And I mean that with every ounce of my being. Nor will I ever talk to my sister again, but that's another soapbox I'm not getting on today.

"Then let. It. Go. For good, Sarah. Don't let Daniel, or your bitch of a sister, undermine your happiness and your future. Liam wants you. You want him. Just see where it goes. Don't be afraid anymore, sweetheart. Let him in."

The hug Raina wraps me in is so comforting. She is more of a sister than my real one will ever be. She holds me while I cry-a little for Sydnee, Daniel, and our broken relationship, but mostly for the loss of my baby. Deep down, this is what hurts the most. This is the pain that's raw and real, that will leave scars on my heart for the rest of my life.

But without a doubt, I know I need to move on with my life. Up until this point, I never let myself hope for something more with a man. But starting today, my life will no longer be a revolving door for men just looking to have a good time for a night or two. Enough is enough. It's time to take control of my own happiness, and maybe that starts with Liam.

Chapter Fourteen

LIAM

faint knocking sound on the door at five o'clock sharp tells me Sarah is here and she didn't freak out and cancel. Honestly, I'm a bit surprised at that. She is one skittish chick when it comes to relationships after her dickhead of an ex and her sister screwed her over. Two pieces of shit, if you ask me.

Upon opening the door, I see bright green eyes, her gorgeous smile, and her posture is, in all honesty, more relaxed than it's ever been around me. She's literally bouncing on her toes, holding an apple pie, and hanging off her arm is a bag with a container of vanilla ice cream. It's like Jekyll and Hyde here. Good Lord, she's, like, glowing or some shit, genuinely happy to be here and doesn't even blink an eye when I answer the door. No hesitation. No awkwardness. No nervousness. She just barges in my apartment like this is the most welcoming place she's ever entered. Like she belongs here, and honest to God, it's the most satisfying feeling but catches me completely off guard.

Her standoffish attitude toward relationships has had me

going over conversations in my head and planning what to do to win her over. Christ, my head's spinning like a fucking fidget spinner after seeing her, and now I have to go to Plan B, which there is no Plan B, so what the hell do I do now?

"Here's some pie and ice cream for dessert. It's home-made. Well, the pie is anyway," she says, waving her hand all around. "I bought the ice cream at the grocery store on my way over here. I hope you like apple. The ice cream is vanilla. God, this pie smells so good, doesn't it? And is that chicken too? Mmmm."

And she fucking moans. Shit. Why do women do that? Do they not know how sexual that sounds to men?

I'm still standing, holding onto the door knob, staring at her like she's some kind of alien creature that's taken over Sarah's body. It's like the game, Never Have I Ever. Never have I ever seen Sarah this happy and relaxed with me.

I try to shake all the jumbled thoughts out of my head and play catch up.

"Okay. Good. Good. You brought pie." I stumble over these six simple words like an idiot. You'd think, after so many years with two sisters I'd know a little something about the female mind. Women's emotions run the gamut from Mary Poppins to Satan or some variation in the middle. One could emerge at any moment, and it's anyone's guess as to which it will be. Men are left to handle the fallout. But in all honesty, that's one of the things that makes women endearing. It just is what it is.

"Do you want the pie in the fridge or what, Liam? The ice cream is gonna melt if you don't stop standing there and get it in the freezer." Her hand goes to her hip and her smile gets bigger.

"Um. Yeah. Let's get it put away." Finally, I'm returning to normal.

Sarah follows me into the small kitchen where sautéed chicken and vegetables are on the stove, with rice almost ready to serve. She starts to help with the meal and I immediately sit her on the stool near the countertop, because she's my company tonight and that means it's her night to be pampered. She has to go back to school tomorrow and I'm quite certain teaching twenty kids that are only seven years old is likely akin to herding squirrels. Nearly impossible.

The wine is chilling in the fridge, so I get it out and pour us two glasses. Sauvignon Blanc was the suggestion from the bartender at Sam's when I asked what to get. I don't mind the taste of wine at all, but knowing which wine goes with chicken or steak or any other meal is beyond my realm of knowledge. Too complicated for me. Personally, just give me a beer or a Jack and Coke, and I'm fine. I stop for a second, remember Sarah's last rendezvous with Jack and Coke, and chuckle to myself.

"You look beautiful sitting here in my kitchen," I say, taking a few steps toward where she's sitting. "Did you have a good workout with Raina today?"

"I did," she says, twirling the stem of her wine glass in her fingers while I twirl her hair. I think that might just be my second most favorite thing to do with her. "We walked and talked. Good conversation."

"Anything you care to share?"

"Sorted out a lot. Gave a lot of thought to what's happening between us."

"Anything you care to share?"

Sarah laughs as I repeat the question, but to be honest, I'd love to know exactly what she sorted. I mean, the way she bopped in here tonight, I kinda have an idea, but I'd love to hear it straight from her beautiful, pink lips.

"Well, I think I've been holding myself back a little from

having any kind of relationship because of the past. After Daniel, I felt like relationships weren't worth the aggravation. They had an end date. In a way, that's like allowing someone else to be in control my happiness more than I am. Part of my issue is Daniel and Sydnee. Trusting is hard for me, as I'm sure you've figured out," she says, closing her eyes and looking down, "but unless I want to live the rest of my life with no real attachments to anyone, I'm going to have to make some changes."

"Question number one, what's the other part of the issue? And question two, are you considering us as an 'us'?" I say, making quotes in the air.

"Well, the other part of my issue is something I just need to get past. So, no need to worry about it. And as far as question two goes, I think *you've* told me in no uncertain terms that there *is* an 'us.'" She also uses air quotes. Her eyes squint a little, but her smirk shows she's not bothered so much by my recently emerging alpha side.

"I have. But you also need to know that if you're not all in, I'll back off. I don't want to pressure you into anything. You need to be open and willing to accept what's going on between us. Admit to yourself that there's an attraction here and it's more than just physical."

"And I have. So, what I'm saying is that I'd really like to...date...exclusively. I mean, you. Date *you* exclusively." And skittish Sarah is back. This time, though, I love what she's saying.

"Thank God. There for a minute, I thought you meant date someone else."

She laughs, and it lights up the room. What a complete surprise she has been tonight. This is exactly what I want, and I want it with her. I'm not under any illusion that everything will be smooth sailing from here on out. She's going to have her moments, so I just need to be aware of that and be ready to reassure her who I am and who I'm not, and what I want out of this relationship.

After dinner is over, we take our wine to the sofa and I turn on the television. I'm a huge sports fan and watching it on my sixty-inch wall mount is perfect. We settle on a college basketball game and snuggle on the couch, like a real couple would do after dinner. I feel like I need to watch something manly on ESPN to get my balls back, because all this talk of relationships and feelings conjures up images of Cole telling me how pussy-whipped I am. Oddly enough, I think I'm okay with that.

Sarah's head is leaning against my shoulder and not long after she settles in, her breathing becomes slow and even. She's asleep. Watching her sleep seems a bit stalker-ish, but I can't help it. Her face is relaxed and her body molds into mine as if we're one person. My hand threads its way through her hair, twisting and twirling it, feeling the softness of it.

The buzzing of my cell phone interrupts the moment. I gently ease off the sofa and snag my phone to answer it. It's Roman. My stomach flips, just for a moment, then I answer.

"Hey, Roman. What's up, man?" I try not to be too loud so I don't wake Sarah.

"Just got off the phone with my dad. He loves the videos I sent him from the bar the other night. Especially the originals. Says you've got a gift for lyrics and songwriting. Some of the best he's heard."

"Wow. I'm glad to hear that. Did he say anything else?"

"Yeah. He's going to have his secretary give you a call. He'd like for you and Cole to make a trip to Nashville if you could. He may have someone there who may possibly be interested."

"Shit. That was fast. When would this happen?"

"He said the woman he wants you to talk to is out of town

for the next two weeks, so she could meet with you when she gets back. That sound like it'll work for you? I know you've got the bar to manage as well."

"Should be okay, man. We hired a bar manager, and we're getting another bartender too. I'll pass this along to Cole."

"Sounds good. Dad's secretary will be calling soon. Good luck with all this."

"I appreciate it. Talk soon."

I sit down, pulling Sarah back against me. My head rests against the back of the sofa but my mind is anything but restful. The wheels are turning and all of a sudden, I'm thinking that maybe this might be the opportunity Cole and I had been looking for, signing to a record label or getting an opportunity to do some songwriting for some of the best artists in the business. Then I think about the bar and how all that would play out. We couldn't just leave Zane to run the whole thing. He's got Samantha now to manage the place, but us leaving would leave him way too short-handed. Could we hire another person or two? No, that cuts into profits and the bar is Zane's only form of income.

"Who was that?" I hear Sarah's yawning, sleepy voice.

There's also Sarah to consider. We're finally getting to a point where she's let her guard down some, so this news would not be welcomed as far as she's concerned. But it's only a meeting. Nothing will probably come out of it anyway. I'm sure this woman has meetings with better musicians than us.

"Just Roman. You want to stay here tonight?" Changing the subject quickly is in my best interest because I can't have that conversation with her tonight. Not already. She's just now beginning to open up.

"I've got to get up for school tomorrow. But, um...I could set the alarm on my phone, get up a little earlier, and go home to get ready."

"Sounds like a good plan to me. You should've brought an overnight bag with you, with all your hair stuff and make-up and brushes and shit. All your clothes. Come to think of it, you would have needed a large suitcase."

"Shut up!" she shrieks, slapping at my shoulder. "That would have been pretty presumptuous of me, now wouldn't it?"

"You were a foregone conclusion, baby. I knew you'd give in to me soon enough. I mean, look at all this," I joke, as I swipe my hand from my head down my body. I grab her around the waist and tickle, her hands flailing wildly and her feet kicking as I get up from the sofa and hoist her up over my shoulder, carrying her into my bedroom. My hand smacks her ass and she stills.

"Settle."

She lets a small giggle out, then relaxes.

Gently, she slides down off my shoulder, rubbing her body against mine the entire way down. When her feet hit the floor, she looks up at me, both hands on my face, rubbing her thumbs along my cheek. Her touch is so gentle, so soothing.

"You want me all in, so I'm all in, Liam. You've been nothing but kind to me, and an amazing friend the past several months. I've always felt something more with you, but it took me this long for my head to catch up with my heart. So, yeah, I'm all in."

Those two words, *all in*, give me a sense of peace I didn't realize I needed.

Finally, I've got her. She's mine.

It doesn't take me long to walk her backward so she's sitting on the bed and I'm standing over her, looking down at the most beautiful girl in the world. My girl.

"Scoot back."

She does as she's told, and my knee eases onto the bed

right between her legs. I lean over, causing her to fall back so she's lying flat. My body covers hers as her arms wrap around me. I don't feel her usual hesitation. I feel her resolve. I feel her giving herself to me completely.

We lay like that, kissing, running our hands along each other's bodies, giving in to each other, knowing where this is leading. I want her to feel my strength and understand that, without a doubt, I will take care of her, always.

Her clothes are in the way of what I want, so I make short work of removing them. She lays naked, on my bed, waiting for me.

Jesus, I could look at her like this all day long. Stunning. So sexy. Reaching behind my head, I pull my shirt off, tossing it on the floor. Her hands settle on my chest, her fingertips gently running along my abs.

"You're so...fit. Your abs. They're so..."

"Sexy?"

She giggles. "Yes. Yes, they are."

"There's more to me than just this chiseled body, sweetheart."

"Oh, there definitely is." Her fingertips continue touching me and I can feel the heat every time they glide across my skin. "Your body, your music, your voice. It's like the trifecta."

Now it's my turn to laugh. "What about my mind?"

"Well, I guess that too." She smiles lovingly at me.

I smirk at her comment then grab her hands, pinning them above her head. "Enough talking. I'm getting tired of waiting for you."

Sarah's mouth opens in surprise and I quickly cover it with mine, kissing her relentlessly, all the while holding her hands firm on the soft mattress.

"Hands stay there. Be still."

"Okay," she whispers, almost breathless, eyes wide.

My lips make their way to her neck, licking and sucking,

taking my time. She lays perfectly still, breathing heavily. There was a time when I didn't really understand how to take care of a woman physically, or even emotionally. I know better now, and as I make my way to those gorgeous tits, I keep in mind how much pleasure a woman gets just from foreplay. It isn't a time to rush. Getting inside of her is the end goal, so there's a sense of urgency, but I take my time, appreciating every sigh and every moan she makes along the way, because I'm the one who caused those. I'm the one who will take her there. Right now, I'm in charge of her pleasure.

My fingers graze across her hardened nipples, pinching ever so slightly. So much for laying still. Her back arches and a shiver breaks out, moving down the length of her body.

"Good?"

"So good."

The assault on her body continues as my tongue caresses her skin from her breasts down to her center, while my hands massage up and down along her sides. One swipe of my tongue through her slit and she nearly comes from that alone. Stopping briefly gives her a moment to relax before I begin again. Her legs spread wider, and her hands grip the pillows. Within minutes, she comes, her legs trembling, stomach clenching and back arching, every molecule of her being wrapped up in a package of pleasure.

"Liam...Liam...oh, God."

She rides the wave of her orgasm all the way to the end, crashing with a deep sigh.

My tongue grazes its way back up her body, kissing, licking, feeling the small aftershocks of her orgasm. Quickly, I remove my jeans, my rock-hard cock finally set free. Two pumps with my fist and I'm ready for her.

"You ready, baby?"

"Now, Liam. I need you now," she whimpers, reaching for me with desperation.

There is no way on Earth I can enter her slowly. I'm so primed and ready, I can't get in that tight body soon enough. One push and I'm inside paradise. Her walls tighten around my cock and my eyes close in pure, unfiltered pleasure. This isn't going to last, I can feel that already.

My movements slow, attempting to prolong the inevitable, but she grabs my hips, moving me, taking what she needs. I love this about her. She doesn't hold back. She takes. She takes from me because she feels safe.

The pace quickens, and soon we're both racing towards the end result. When we hit that high together, our eyes lock and we connect on a level I've never reached with another human being before in my life.

She is the one.

After that moment passes between us, we both collapse, lying side by side, exhausted.

"I'll be right back," she whispers as she crawls out of bed, heading towards the bathroom.

I roll to my side, waiting and watching for the bathroom door to open. A few minutes pass and she still hasn't come out. I silently make my way to the bathroom door, easing it open just a bit. Sarah stands there in front of the mirror with tears in her eyes.

Shit.

"Sweetheart?"

"I'm okay. I'm good." She wipes the tears from her eyes and turns to face me, pulling me in for a hug. "There's never been a time when I've felt that connection before. God, Liam, this feels so real to me."

"It is real. This is us, and it's good."

"Yeah. It is. That look right before...you know? I've never ever had a man look at me like that, with so much emotion. I kinda panicked, I think." Those shimmering green eyes find mine. "Us." That's all she says, shaking her head.

"Yeah. Us."

I pick her up and walk her back to bed, laying her down. Climbing in beside her, I reach to pull her over to me. I want her skin touching mine. I want her arms and legs wrapped around me like a ribbon. I want her. Forever.

Chapter Fifteen

SARAH

In the grand scheme of things, being in a relationship with Liam shouldn't be a big deal. He's so handsome, kind, and caring. He's honest to a fault, and did I say handsome? For me, though, this is a very big deal. I'd like to say I'm completely at ease and totally comfortable with it, but in all honesty, I'm a little bit nervous. I do want this, but I've just always resigned myself to hook-ups and one-night stands after the shit that went down with Daniel.

But it feels good. It feels natural and real, and I know it's just a matter of giving myself time to adjust to being with him.

My phone alarm goes off earlier than I normally set it because I need to haul ass home and get ready for school. Peeling myself from Liam and rolling over toward the small stand where my phone is dinging relentlessly, I pull the sheet just a bit too far, and when I turn to make sure I didn't wake Liam, I see my man, sprawled on the bed, naked as the day he was born. His hair is tousled, and one arm thrown across his eyes, shielding the bit of light starting to make its way through the slivers of space in the window blinds. What a glorious way to wake up on a workday. That image will be running on the Liam-is-so-fucking-hot highlight reel in my head the entire day.

"Babe, if you don't throw those covers back on me, there will be hell to pay." I chuckle when I look at him, lying there naked, eyes covered, not moving a muscle. Quickly, I throw the sheet across his body covering up all that wicked goodness...the morning hard-on Liam is sporting. Morning wood is a definite thing, and my man has it in spades. I only wish I had the time to take care of that for him.

My clothes are strewn about the floor after last night's exploits, and I'm grabbing at them so I can get home. Suddenly, strong arms encompass me from behind, and the morning wood? Still there, and pressed up against me so sinfully, I halfway consider taking the day off.

"Are you trying to make me late with that...cock all up in my business?"

"All up in your business? Let me show you exactly what I can do with this cock that's all up in your business," he whispers in my ear, biting at the lobe. Liam's hands reach around and his callused fingertips grab my breasts, flicking at my nipple like the strings he plucks on his guitar.

"You got five minutes."

I'm once again tossed over Liam's shoulder and taken back to his bed.

Thirty minutes later, I'm rushing out the door, knowing I'll be late for school. But no regrets on my part. Not one.

Chapter Sixteen

LIAM

"Listen to me, Cole. Stop and listen."

"Okay, man. I'm ready. Hit me." So much energy.

"Roman, Tatum's boyfriend, said his old man's secretary is gonna call us to set up a time to meet with another executive. She's out of town till late next week, but he wants us to meet with her when she gets back. Looks like we're headed to Nashville in two weeks or so, but we've gotta talk with Zane, man. We can't leave him high and dry, ya know?"

I've been on the phone with Cole, trying to explain this shit to him now for twenty minutes. It's like he can't even comprehend what I'm trying to say. He's rattled off terms like contracts, hot women, concerts, and hot women again. It's like trying to explain the concept of the Universe to a five-year-old. Cole is nothing if not energetic, and he's just as psyched about this as I am, but, in the end, we were both in agreement that we've got to meet with Zane.

"I'll give him a call and see if we can catch up at the bar in about an hour, if that works for you?" Cole asks.

"Yep, that works. See ya then."

Every time I think of Nashville and the opportunities that may present themselves there, my mind circles right back to Sarah. She has to know. I can't just up and leave for a few days without telling her. I just have to figure out the right way to do it.

Damn. Why did this have to happen now? Shit like this just doesn't happen to everyone, and we can't let it pass us by. I'm sure she'll understand, right? She knows how much my music means to me. I've been writing songs since I was ten years old and to have the opportunity to break into the music business with Cole would totally rock. Even if it's just songwriting, which is my passion anyway. I can write songs from anywhere.

See? The more I talk this out in my head, the easier it all sounds. Everything will work out. I just need to chill and have more confidence in Sarah. She'll be fine.

"I DON'T WANT either of you to worry about anything. Samantha and I will cover here. We just need to speed up on getting another full-time bartender and I'd also suggest another server as well."

"We want you to be sure, Zane, because we're invested in this place too. It'll only be a few days and until we know exactly what this lady is looking for, it's hard to even guess what's gonna happen in the future. But I, for one, can tell you that I'm not bailing on you. We're in this together, yeah?"

"Absolutely," says Cole. "I know we've always kinda had in the back of our minds that someday we'd get a break in the business, but that was years ago. I wanna know what this woman is thinking, where she sees us in the business. It's so much to think about right now that my head is spinning."

"S'all good, man. Just hear what this woman has to say

and go from there. We'll be back here thinkin' all the good thoughts." Zane turns my way and I know exactly what's on his mind before he says a word. "What did Sarah say about it?"

"Haven't said anything to her yet. She's so damn guarded that I'm having a hard time figuring out exactly what to say. She's had some bad luck with men in the past, and I sure don't want to be added to *that* shit list."

Zane laughs, smacking his knee. "She's a spitfire, that one. But seriously, she needs to know. The more open and honest you can be with her, the better."

"Look at you, all feelings and shit," I say, taking a drink of soda. Never thought I'd see the day when *that* man talked feelings. He's had a tough life, but Raina seems to settle him, keeps him grounded. She's his rock.

"All I know is Sarah is Raina's best friend, and what affects Sarah affects my girl, which in turn, affects me. So, don't screw her over. Raina and I are in a good place and don't need shit messin' that up."

"You've got nothin' to worry about. She's gonna be fine. But don't say anything to her until I figure out how to first."

Cole and I are playing just one set tonight, during a Ladies Only Happy Hour thing that Cole dreamed up. He loves his women and they flock to him for whatever reason. He's a good-lookin' shit, but such a manwhore. But the way he looks at Samantha when he thinks no one's watching? Well *that* tells me sure as shit he's more interested in her than he lets on. Not sure what her story is. Popped up out of nowhere, looking for a job. Damn good at what she does, though.

I shoot a text to Sarah asking her to meet me here later on, and she agrees to stop by. I need to run some errands first, so I head out to get that taken care of.

THE BAR IS PACKED by the time I get back, and there is Cole, sandwiched between two blondes. Complete opposites of Samantha. My eyes bounce back and forth between Cole and Samantha, and I can most definitely say that if looks could kill, Cole and those blondes would be toast. This is gonna get good.

"Hey, Sam." I squeeze my way between two regulars here at the bar, trying to get her attention. "Hey, Sam. Grab me a bottle of my water in the cooler, would ya?"

"Sure thing," she says, reaching down to snag a cold one for me. "Busy tonight, huh? Good for tips though."

"Absolutely. Cole's Ladies Only Happy Hour, or whatever the hell he calls it, is a good idea, don't you think?"

She rolls her eyes, turning her nose up in disgust as she shakes her head. "Yeah. He's a real genius, that one." She hands me my water then goes back to taking orders on the other side of the bar, a bit of a scowl on her pretty face. If I didn't know better, I would say I've just hit a nerve. Interesting. Physically speaking, Sam is not the kind of woman Cole usually goes for, so his attraction to her is a bit unexpected. She's a beautiful woman, sure, just more reserved and down-to-Earth than the bimbos that typically throw themselves at him. A bit on the shorter side, curves for miles, and more of a "jeans and tee" kind of girl. Sweet as shit, though.

I make my way through the crowd toward the stage, stopping along the way to catch up with a few people who come to see us regularly. When Sarah comes through the door, I motion for her to head up to the table I have reserved for us near the stage. When I'm in the zone, playing my guitar and singing one of her favorite songs, I love looking into the crowd to see her smiling that beautiful smile that's reserved for only me. I fuckin' own that smile. Damn, I'm a lucky man.

Chapter Seventeen

SARAH

Liam's body is perfection. No, really, it is. My hands have grazed over every single chiseled inch of perfection on that beautiful, toned man, and not one flaw. So, the boyish grin he flashes, along with the quick wink, makes me giddy as hell as I sit down at our table. I don't do giddy. Except now, I quite possibly do. However, I'm twenty-five, not sixteen.

He and Cole are entertaining the crowd here tonight at what Cole has dubbed Ladies Only Happy Hour. Every other bar in America calls it Ladies' Night, but Cole had to be different. It's cute that he thinks his idea is original. So only the ladies get half-priced drinks. He calls it a win-win. He gets to sit on stage, drinking and singing, all the while watching the women stagger in by the dozens, ready to fawn all over him. Damn creepers. It's interesting, though, that tonight his attention is drawn more to the new bartender, Samantha, than the rest of the women.

This table, this spot near the stage, is where I have been sitting the last several months when I come to the bar with Raina if the guys are working. It's just our spot. However, tonight it seems different somehow, and I don't know what to make of that. It feels good. It feels right.

It's a little unnerving watching some of the women here making eyes at Liam and making advances toward him. It's understandable, really. I mean, just look at him. But never once does he take advantage of that, nor does he flaunt it in my face by flirting with any of them. He never has. It's like I've always been his in one way or another. He's always wanted more with me, and he's finally worn me down.

The two of them are playing one set tonight, which is fine by me since it's a school night and I need to be home at a decent hour. They're finishing up their last song, an original that Liam wrote about love and second chances, and in a few minutes, after the equipment is cleared off the small stage, Liam will be all mine. Makes my heart flutter.

Honestly. A giddy, fluttering heart. When I think long and hard about it, I don't ever remember having these same feelings for Daniel when we were together. My lips upturn in a smile. He was the one to let me go, and if he never had, I would have never met Liam. Next time I see that piece of shit, I'll be sure to thank him for all that.

Thinking of Daniel this time doesn't make me frown or piss me off. He's now just part of a past that I'm moving on from, forgetting about, because he's not worth it. Neither is my sister. All just a distant memory. Moments that have passed, moments I've learned so much from.

A delicate touch to my shoulder makes me jump nearly out of my seat, and I spin around to find Liam there, almost knocking him over. "What in the ever-loving hell is it with you all? Can we *not* try to scare the shit out of me anymore?"

"It's just so cute, babe. You're all focused on whatever it is you're thinking, and when I touched you, your eyes kinda like bugged out of your head, and your hands came up to your cheeks," he jokes, then leans in to whisper in my ear.

"And it's just about the most adorable look I've ever seen." His voice is deep and raspy from singing. My eyes close, thinking of that sexy voice in the bedroom. Suddenly, it's very warm in here, and I think a breath of fresh air, or a drink, or even a garden hose to the face would be nice right about now.

"Babe?"

"I could just use another, um, drink."

"I could get one for you, or we could head out. I know you've got school tomorrow."

"Let's go then. Just let me catch up with Raina first to let her know I'm leaving."

I grab for my purse to go find Raina at the bar with Zane when my cell phone buzzes, which is odd for this time of night. I look at the number and instantly sigh when I see my sister's name on the caller ID.

Decline.

Within minutes, my phone buzzes again and I know if I don't answer her, she'll just keep calling. Whatever she wants, she had better be quick about it because I'm thinking I've got some really hot sex coming tonight.

"What is it, Sydnee?"

"Oh, thank God. Sarah, it's Dad. He's been taken to the hospital."

"What? What happened?"

"Mom said he got really short of breath, had a hard time breathing when they were putting boxes in the attic. He started having sharp pains in his chest. He sat down to rest for a minute, but then the pains came back, so they called the ambulance."

"Where are you?"

"We're at the hospital now. Are you going to come?"

"I'm on my way."

"Oh, thank God. I need to see you too."

"To see Dad, Sydnee. I'm coming to see Dad."

"Sarah..."

"Don't. Just don't. I'm on my way."

The nervousness in my voice clues Liam in to the fact that something is definitely wrong because before I can even make a move, he's right there.

"What's going on?"

"Liam, do you think you could drive me to the hospital? Dad's been taken there. That was Sydnee, and she said Mom had to call the ambulance. They're there now."

"Absolutely, sweetheart. Let's go. I'll text Zane and Cole later, so they know what's going on," he says as we hurriedly make our way to his car. Within minutes, we're on the highway, headed to the hospital.

The fact that I'm going to be face-to-face with Sydnee, and most likely Daniel, after so long gets pushed to the back of my mind. I need to focus on Dad, and I'm upset that neither he nor Mom told me he had been sick, but then again, I haven't called much either.

"What's going through that head of yours, babe?" Liam reaches over to take hold of my hand, gently rubbing his thumb along my wrist. It's soothing and calming.

I consider that this will be the first time Liam will meet my family. My mom and dad don't even know I'm dating again, although Mom finds a way to weave the dating subject into the short conversations we do have occasionally. I was so broken after what happened that I barely make a phone call or two every few weeks to check in. I've never asked about Sydnee, and I sure as hell never asked about Daniel. The only reason I don't wish for his demise is because of my niece, Londyn. She needs a mother *and* a father so I feel somewhat bad plotting his death. Well, that's a tad dramatic, but you know what I mean. I've only ever been with her when she's been at Mom and Dad's, when both Daniel and Sydnee were working. My God, parts of my life are a mess.

"Right now, I feel like shit for not going to see Mom and Dad more often. I always felt like they overlooked all the shit Sydnee did to me because they see her, Daniel, and Londyn all the time. It's like it made no difference to them at all. I guess I'm mostly feeling guilty, though." I turn my head to look out the window, watching headlights and signs and other cars we pass on the way to Raleigh. "Jesus, I hope we make it there in time before anything happens," I whisper, holding back the stinging tears in my eyes.

"Everything is gonna be fine, darlin'. We'll be there before you know it. You need to relax and put the other two out of your mind. You're going there for your dad, not to see them."

I lean my head back against the headrest in Liam's car and close my eyes, trying to shut out visions of the worst possible scenario playing out when I get there. Deep breaths in through my nose, out through my mouth.

"Keep breathing, babe. Keep yourself calm."

"You know, it's much easier to breathe when I'm with you, Liam. Just by being here with me you make me feel so much better."

A squeeze to my hand, a wink and a smile does more for my nerves that nearly anything else.

IT ISN'T LONG at all before we arrive at the hospital, and I'm dropped off at the emergency entrance while Liam scours the parking lot for a space. The doors to the ER glide open instantly as I rush in, seeing my mom sitting in the waiting room, head down, resting it in her hands.

"Mom."

She's up from her chair, her motherly arms wrapping me

in a hug. Initially, I think of how much I've missed this. Mom and I were close once. I guess we all were, all four of us. As Sydnee got older, Mom seemed to pay more attention to her and all the drama she'd engage in. It was like Mom got sucked into it all, leaving me to fend for myself. Right now, though, I need to put all that aside.

"How is he? Has the doctor been out?"

"Not yet. They took him back immediately. They hooked him up to do an EKG or something like that. I don't know anything more."

"He's in good hands here, Mom. He's gonna be okay. He's stubborn, you know." It's hard trying to integrate some humor in such a serious situation, but if it helps Mom feel more at ease, I'll do whatever I need to.

"That he is, Sarah. I'm so glad you're here."

"Oh, Mom. Where else would I be? It's Dad."

"I know, sweetie. But you don't come around much. Dad misses you. *I* miss you." Her eyes are rimmed red and she looks pale. I've got to do better. I can't have them worry like this.

"Let's just focus on getting Daddy better. We'll deal with everything else later."

Just as Mom and I are sitting down, Liam comes through the automatic doors, walking toward us. He looks tired, but I know there is nowhere else he'd be right now. I stand, taking his hand, pulling him toward me.

"What's happening now, babe?"

"The doctors are running tests right now. That's all we know."

"Sarah, who's this?" I hear my mom's voice from behind me.

"Mom, this is Liam. Liam, this is my mom."

He reaches for her hand, only my mom doesn't take it. Instead, she pulls him in for a hug.

"Thank you for bringing our Sarah." She's a good eight inches shorter than Liam and reaches up with her hand, patting his cheek. "Thank you."

"No problem, Mrs. Witten. I hope everything's okay."

Before Mom can answer, Sydnee walks around the corner with drinks from the cafeteria. She stops when she looks up and sees me with Liam and Mom. After a moment's pause, she comes over to us, handing Mom her drink.

"You're here...um...good." She stumbles through those three words like I'm a stranger.

"I'm here." My response is clipped, short. I don't have energy for her right now.

Just then, the ER doors open and a doctor heads our way. At first glance, he shows no expression. Not pity, worry, or anything that would indicate my dad is in serious trouble. It's oddly comforting.

"Mrs. Witten."

Mom turns around and I find her taking a step, nearly collapsing. The doctor grabs for her, helping her to the chair. She's exhausted and worried, and rightly so. This is nothing short of overwhelming for her. Dad is never sick, so I'm sure she's nearly at her wits' end.

"Oh my. I'm so sorry. Turned around too fast, is all. Is he...is he okay?"

"We need to be sure you're okay. Give yourself a second."

"Oh, goodness. I'm just worried. That's all." Mom tries to make light, waving her hand around, implying we're not to worry about her.

"If you want to be checked out, you're in the right place."

"I'm fine. But I need to know about my husband. Is he going to be okay?"

"Well, right now, he is alert and based on the information from the EKG, it appears he's had a heart attack."

"Oh, God." Terror makes its way into Mom's voice. I've not ever heard it before.

"Mrs. Witten, he's stable. We're going to take him to the cath lab right now for a cardiac catheterization. It's going to allow us to see the coronary arteries better to determine where the blockages are."

"Blockages. That's why he couldn't breathe, right? And the chest pain too," Mom interrupts.

"Yes. We'll handle this one of two ways. Either he'll require coronary artery bypass, or we may be able to treat with stents. Once we get all the information we need, I'll be back to let you know, okay?"

"Dr. Donovan, please take care of him." My mom weeps, holding onto Sydnee's arm and taking my hand.

"Mrs. Witten, he's getting the best possible care. Why don't you all go up to the family waiting room on the fifth floor. That's where we'll be bringing your husband once he's out of the cath lab."

"That would be wonderful. Thank you."

Dr. Donovan turns to leave but hesitates a moment. "Mrs. Witten, you need to rest once you get upstairs, okay?"

"We'll see that she does," I reply.

Mom turns to me with a sad smile. "I'm so glad you're here, sweetheart."

"Let's go up to the waiting room. We can get some coffee there, and I'm sure the chairs are more comfortable. These seats are hard on the ass."

"Oh, Sarah, your language," Mom says with half a laugh.

We gather our things, ready to head to the elevators. Looking toward the doors when I hear the swoosh of them opening, my knees nearly buckle, and I fall, probably not so gracefully, back in the chair when I see Daniel come inside. It's been well over a year since I've seen him, and I feel as though the wind has literally been knocked from my lungs.

All the memories come crashing back like a tidal wave. Unwanted and damaging. Sydnee walks toward him, and he takes hold of her, wrapping her in a hug, comforting her like he used to do for me. It's when he pulls away from her that he catches sight of me, and the glare when he sees me is filled with anger and regret. He's angry? Why should he be angry? He got exactly what he wanted. Well, fuck him. And fuck Sydnee. She can have him.

And why the hell can't I breathe again? It's really a simple process.

It doesn't take Liam but a minute to realize this is Daniel because, before I can make another move, Liam is at my side, arm around my back, looking at me and telling me with his eyes that I'm okay. That he's got me. His hand comes to my face, and the touch alone not only calms my anxious nerves, but also shows Daniel that I am Liam's.

"He's not your problem anymore, sweetheart. Let it go," he whispers, so no one else can hear the words that bring me peace. This man is so much more than Daniel will ever be.

Together, we all make our way to the elevators and up to the family waiting room in the heart unit of the hospital. The elevator ride is silent, tense, and I can feel Liam's agitation at being this close to Daniel. Fortunately, we find much more comfortable chairs when we reach the room, which makes me glad that Mom will have an easier time resting here. The jitters I feel every time I look at Daniel only worsen when I sit still for too long, yet pacing around the waiting room, trying to ignore his presence, is making me weary. I'm too anxious.

"Mom, Liam and I are going for a drink. Do you need anything?" Liam takes his cue and gets up from his chair to walk with me, thankful, I'm sure, to escape some of the tension. It doesn't take a rocket scientist to figure out he's furious, and the longer he sits there, the angrier he gets. His fists clench, and there's a storm in his dark eyes.

"No, sweetheart. I'm fine. Maybe check with Sydnee or Daniel to see if they need something, though."

"With all due respect, Mrs. Witten, I think Daniel and Sydnee are capable of getting what they need. Are you sure you don't need anything?"

"I'm fine, honey."

"Come on, Sarah. You need a break." Liam's voice cracks in frustration.

Liam's comment doesn't even register with Mom. Snide, off-the-cuff comments I've made about Daniel and Sydnee being together after he dumped me when I was pregnant never have.

As we turn to walk out of the family waiting room, Sydnee jumps from her chair and reaches for my elbow, trying to stop me, as Daniel calls out for me to wait.

Liam quickly interrupts, "I said Sarah needs a break. Did you not hear me? Was that not clear enough for you?"

"Liam, it's okay. Let's go. They're not worth the trouble," I say, taking his hand to usher him out into the hallway. He's overly-protective right now, and as sexy as that is, he needs to back off because I know Daniel, and he will instigate and add fuel to an already burning fire.

We walk down the long corridor to the lounge area where we find soda and snack machines. Before I can tell him what I'd like, he spins me around, taking my face in his hands. He tilts his head to the side, and kisses me with a softness and gentleness that calms my racing heart. Our lips fit perfectly together, like mine were always made for kissing his.

'Thank you," I whisper. "No one has ever taken up for me like that before." Our lips are a hair's breadth apart.

"I won't let them hurt you again, sweetheart. Ever."

"I know."

"Do you really? Do you know I would go to the ends of the earth to protect you?"

Without hesitating, I reply, "Yes. Yes, I do. And I lo...I mean, I'm truly grateful for that."

Shit. That almost came out. I can't tell him I love him. I mean, I think I do, but it's too soon. He'll feel like he has to say it back and what if he doesn't really feel that way yet? Maybe he never will. Although, after what he just did for me back there, I'm inclined to believe that maybe he does. But, no. I'm not ready to go there. Not after how emotional this evening has been. So, I just let it go and push those feelings to the back of my conscience where they belong. They can't be out in the open yet.

"That was a whole lot of thinking going on in those few seconds of silence, Sarah. Care to fill me in?"

"I'm just glad that you're here." My hand reaches up to his, grasping his wrists. "I couldn't have faced that alone, not with the way my emotions are all over the place right now."

"You owe Daniel and Sydnee nothing. Concentrate on your dad and mom. Focus your efforts there and let everyone else around you do what they need to do for themselves. You're gonna be okay, babe. You know that, right?"

"Yeah. I'm starting to believe that. The initial shock of seeing him was difficult, but it's over now. He and Sydnee are still together, and they have Londyn. So now, it's a matter of keeping it in the past where it belongs. I've got to be strong for Mom. She's the one who needs me. Not them."

I'm decidedly better off now than I was just a few short minutes ago. I'm back in control, and when I have to face them again, which will happen multiple times over with Dad in the hospital, I can think back to this moment right here with Liam and feel the strength inside of me to handle it.

"Let's get some drinks and head back. The doctor should

be coming in to let us know your dad's condition and I know you'll want to hear all that. Your mom's going to need someone to help her understand everything and to make any decisions she might need to make."

We exit the small lounge, and before we make it to the waiting room, Liam stops me.

"He gets nothing else, sweetheart. He had you once and didn't care enough to see what an amazing woman you were, still are, and he let you go. He gets nothing understand? Not a tear, not a whimper, nothing."

A barrage of emotions hits me right then, but all I can do is smile. "Nothing," I repeat. "It's just you."

"You bet your sweet ass it's just me. No one else, Sarah." The light smack on my ass is something I'm beginning to look forward to.

We walk hand in hand back into the waiting room, my head held a little higher, my emotions much more under control, and I'm on the arm of the most amazing man I've ever meet. When he says he's got me, he really does.

As soon as we take a seat to wait, the doctor comes into the room with more news about Dad.

Chapter Eighteen

As Dr. Donovan enters the waiting room, Sarah and her mom and Sydnee stand, nervous energy in their stance.

"Good news. We're going to be able to treat your husband with stents. Bypass surgery isn't necessary. We'll take care of that in the cath lab and he'll be in a room in a few hours."

"Oh, thank God." The relief is visible. Sarah lets out a huge breath, holding on to Mrs. Witten as her posture finally begins to loosen. Now, if I could just keep from punching the shit out of Daniel, well then, everything should be fine.

"Since it's early morning, we'll keep him a couple days, then he should be good to go. I will say, he'll need to take it easy for several weeks. There is a cardiac rehab program here for him as well. We can talk about all that later, once we get him to his room."

Sarah's mom thanks the doctor as he leaves, then slumps in the chair, happy tears falling.

THE NEXT TWO hours pass slowly as we wait for the all-clear from the doctor. Sarah's mom is reclined in the oversized chair, eyes closed. She has to be exhausted. Sarah sits with her head on my shoulder, falling in and out of a light sleep.

"Sweetheart, I'm going outside to text Zane, so he can let Raina know how your dad's doing. I'll tell her to pull your classroom plans for the substitute."

"That would be great. I need to talk to Mom for a few minutes anyway." Her voice is quiet and sounds so tired. She yawns as she tries to sit up straighter in the chair.

I look to the other side of the waiting room at Daniel and the intimidating eye contact I give him should make it clear that, in no uncertain terms, he needs to leave Sarah the hell alone. He acts like an entitled piece of shit, as if everyone owes him something. He glares for a moment, then turns away. Pussy. I can't wait to get Sarah the hell out of here away from those two.

"Be right back, babe," I say, kissing her on the cheek.

When I get outside, I take a deep breath and try to calm down. Sarah doesn't need me losing my shit in the middle of all this, so I walk to the car to get her jacket, in case she starts to get cold in the waiting room. Or maybe that's an excuse to walk off some frustration, and a hell of a lot of excess energy. Energy I'd like to use to punch that asshole in the face.

The text goes right through to Zane. A few minutes later, he texts back that he'll update Raina on all that's happened. Their lives are so in sync now, it's amazing. They both deserve that kind of love, that kind of happiness, and it makes me think about Sarah and me being that close one day. A snarky smile covers my face. Yeah, it's like that.

My steps are a little lighter walking back into the hospital. I hit the elevator button and make my way back to Sarah. It's when I step off the elevator that I hear loud, clipped voices, an argument of some kind, coming from the waiting room.

I rush in to find Sarah in tears again, her mom nowhere to be found, and I nearly go fucking ballistic. What in God's name is wrong with these people?

"Sarah," I call out to her. She turns to find me standing in the doorway, ready to kick someone's ass. I walk over to her, take her in my arms, and feel her body shake with sobs.

"What the fuck is wrong with you two?"

"Liam, don't. It's okay."

"You're in fucking tears, Sarah. It's not okay, sweetheart." Furious doesn't even begin to cover how I feel right now, and the moment I turn to face that coward, he takes a few steps back. I hope he understands just how difficult it is for me to refrain from lighting his ass up. "I wanna know what the hell you said to her."

Sarah speaks up before he has a chance to answer. "Daniel, just go. You and Sydnee just go out in the hallway and wait for Mom. They'll only let her with Dad for a little while. You'll need to take her home."

"Sarah, we're not finished this conversation. Not even close," Daniel says, walking toward her.

Both my hands leave Sarah and grab hold of that asshole's shirt. Within seconds, his back is up against the wall and I'm cocked, ready to thump his ass.

"Liam! Stop." I barely register Sarah's voice because in my head I'm thinking of all the ways I can lay him out. "Stop, please."

I let the asshole go and, of course, Sarah's sister is falling all over him, nearly in tears.

"Sydnee, please get him out of here."

Sarah's sister looks at her with a mix of disdain and guilt, and then she walks Daniel out of the waiting room. If I never see those two again, it'll be too soon. I don't even know how to process the fact that Sydnee betrayed Sarah the way she did. I grew up with sisters who were the kindest, most caring, girls I knew. They looked out for each other, even though they were years apart. Neither would have ever thought of stooping so low as to sleep with the other's boyfriend. That shit is just jacked.

"Liam, listen to me. I know you came in on the tail end of all that. What did…what did you hear?"

"All I saw was Daniel getting in your face. I don't need to know what he was saying to know he was pissed. Jesus, Sarah, are you okay?" I wrap her back up in my arms, my lips on her forehead, comforting her as best I can. How much more shit can she possibly take?

"Okay. Good."

"What do you mean, *good*?"

"Just good that, you know, no one got hurt. You need to keep your hands off him. I'd like to half strangle him too, but I've got a niece to think about. That's her dad, whether I like it or not, and Sydnee is her mother. Believe me, it sucks more than you know."

"Why was he so upset?"

"It's nothing. Everyone's nerves are on edge and there was just a disagreement. It's fine."

"I better never hear him raise his voice to you again. Because next time I can't be held responsible if I throat punch that dick."

"Let it go. That's what you tell me, right?"

Easier said than done. There's no time to answer her because Mrs. Witten walks back into the waiting room, thankfully without the other two.

"Your dad's fine and resting. Daniel and Sydnee are leaving, so they'll take me home. Sydnee will bring me back later."

Tears gather in Mrs. Witten's eyes, so much so that the

knots of anger in my stomach begin to untangle and what's left is a feeling of sadness for her. It's so obvious she loves her husband with all her heart. It makes me think about what my mom would do if she no longer had Dad.

"I didn't know they would confront you, Sarah. I'm sorry I told them. I thought they should know. I thought it was time to…Sydnee is having a hard time with–"

What the hell is she talking about? Maybe my sadness for her is misplaced.

"Stop. Don't say another word. We're not having this discussion, Mom." Sarah interrupts her mother, and I'm undecided now as to whether to ask about what upset Sarah so much. Could this night get any worse?

"Liam, could you take me back to the house? I need a shower and a little sleep." She turns to her mom and the usual softness in her eyes is gone. What remains is emptiness, sadness. "Mom, I'll be back late morning. If anything changes, call me right away."

With that, she turns and walks out of the room, not even giving her mom a chance to respond. I need to find out what happened while I was outside texting Zane. Something more went down with Sarah and Daniel in here than what she's telling me. It was more than a simple disagreement that caused that kind of reaction, I can guarantee it, and I want to know what it was. Whatever happened in the past has just resurfaced, because Sarah's face is expressionless, empty, and that worries me. She's shut down completely. And if it weren't for the fact that I just now got her to open up, it wouldn't be so bad. But she's barely hanging on right now by the looks of her. I'm so afraid she'll fall and I'll never get her back.

Chapter Nineteen

SARAH

My tired eyes open slowly to the filtered sunlight streaming through the blinds on the bedroom window. God, it feels as though I just fell asleep. The air in the room feels cool with the ceiling fan on low, but Liam's body is a furnace curled up against mine, warming me, comforting me. He allowed absolutely no space between us last night, holding me as if this were the last time I'd ever stay in his bed again. I'm not certain how to swing this story to make him believe there was nothing going on with Daniel except a pointless argument. In fact, the entire conversation with Daniel really *was* pointless. Daniel was livid that I didn't tell him I was pregnant with his baby then miscarried, but what good would that have done. The fact my mother told him about the miscarriage infuriates me. She had no right to do that, and I will be very interested to hear her reasoning. What I don't need now is sympathy from Daniel or Sydnee, and I sure as hell don't want their pity.

"A lot going on in your mind this morning, babe."

"Worried. About Dad...and Mom," I reply, without turning to face him. His arm is still wrapped around me as tight as a twisted rubber band, and he isn't letting go. There was a time when that would have freaked me out, would have had me bailing without a second thought. Liam is so different. Why can't I trust him with this?

"I need to get up and get ready to head to the hospital." But as soon as I make a move to get up, I'm dragged back to bed, glued to Liam's side.

"There's a conversation that needs to happen. Not right now, because we've got to get going. But, baby, it will happen. You remember I told you that I've got you? I'm not letting go, Sarah, so whatever it is, you can tell me. In fact, you may feel better once you tell me what's going on in that beautiful mind of yours."

It's a bit difficult to focus when Liam's morning wood is sticking me near my ass and his deep, sexy voice is right in my ear. But focus I must because he is not going to let this go.

I totally get that miscarriages happen, I do, and most women are okay in time. It's just that I've felt so guilty for so long because I didn't handle the stress of what Daniel and Sydnee did to me well at all. Anger, betrayal, and heartache were kept bottled inside to the point that I nearly became a different person. People didn't usually describe me as closed off, or moody, or disinterested, but that's what I'd become. I had let the stress of the entire situation control me, so much so that it caused me to lose the baby.

The physician on call the day I ended up in the hospital said stress can be a factor, because women handle stress differently, but it's likely only one part of the reason why I miscarried. Whatever the reason, it happened, and I've always felt responsible for that. The issue now though, is more than just dealing with a miscarriage. So much more.

Then I had the pleasure of being humiliated, on top of everything else when Sydnee and Daniel's relationship came out. So, it festered and festered, but I kept that shit on lock-down, telling no one, getting no help. It's been years of living with this secret, but it's all going to come to blows now because Daniel won't let it go. He isn't the kind to pass along his sympathy and move on. He's going to want to know what happened and why, and all the while, he'll be blaming me.

"I can go to the hospital by myself, Liam. I don't need a babysitter."

"Never said you did, darlin'. But I'm going. We either go together or I'll take my own car, but I'm not letting you go there on your own, knowing your sister and Daniel will be there too."

My phone dings a text message tone and I quickly grab it to check, hoping for good news about Dad. My own heart is happy and relieved when I read Mom's message that the nurses had contacted her to let her know Dad was doing very well. Mom also said Sydnee is taking her to the hospital while Daniel has Londyn at home. She's anxious to see her pappy, but they want to give him a few days of rest before that little spitfire comes around. She's the one regret I have most about limiting my time with the family. I love her to death, no matter who her parents are, but I wish the situation weren't so volatile, which would give me the chance to spend more time with her.

So, Dad's okay for now, thank God, because I'm not ready for him not to be. I'm not at all certain how *I* am doing right now, though. I have to tell Liam and I need to do it before he hears it from Daniel. I'm just not mentally prepared for how he'll take this, because he will look at me differently now, knowing I'd been an irresponsible, pregnant eighteen-year-old.

"That was Mom. She said Dad's doing well and he's rest-ing." The smile is genuine because I couldn't be happier about Dad. It just doesn't reach my eyes because I know the conversation about the past is inevitable. "Let's get ready then because I don't want to be late leaving."

There isn't much in the way of happiness in my voice and the look on Liam's face tells me the inquisition about what is bothering me will continue the length of the late morning ride to the hospital.

＆

WATCHING the scenery pass as we make our way to see Dad doesn't seem to take my mind off anything. Dad, the miscarriage, my relationship with Liam, babies. None of it. It's all swirling around in my head like a tilt-a-whirl ride at the carnival. Back and forth, around and around, until I'm nearly sick to my stomach.

Pulling into the lot at the hospital is a welcome relief from a very quiet and intense ride here. Liam said very little, obviously waiting for me to spill the beans. His one-word answers to the trivial questions I threw out were short and to the point, letting me know his displeasure at me avoiding the elephant in the room-or car, as it is.

Liam and I walk into Dad's room, hand in hand, and I'm so excited to see him sitting up and eating. I try to drop Liam's hand walking into the room, but he's having none of it. There is color back in Dad's face, and he's complaining about the attention, so I know that's a good sign.

"Hey, old man!" I tease.

"Not too old to take you over my knee, little lady." He gives as good as he gets and my frayed nerves begin to calm with the light bantering. I don't miss his eyes locking in on Liam's hand firmly holding mine. He looks back at me with a wink.

"But seriously, Dad, how're you feeling?"

"Like a new man. Not short of breath anymore, feel like I have more energy."

"But no marathons anytime soon, yeah?"

"No princess, no marathons," he answers with a chuckle in his voice.

Liam reaches his hand out and introduces himself to my dad. "Mr. Witten, I'm Liam. Good to meet you, sir, and glad you're feeling better."

"So, you're here with my Sarah, so that must mean you're her..." Dad replies in a questioning tone.

"Boyfriend is a bit childish-sounding, but I guess you could say that's what I am. We've been friends for quite a while and I've finally gotten her to agree to go out with me."

"Well, color me impressed, because Sarah here doesn't go out on dates with anyone these days. You must be a good fella. You take care of her, hear me?"

"Yes, sir. That I can do."

"Jesus, Dad. I *am* in the room, you know. And I do date...a little. Now, can we get back to you? What have the doctors said?"

"I should be out of here tomorrow. Just gonna keep their eye on me a little bit longer, then I'm good to go." Dad's voice turns to a hushed whisper. "Don't tell your momma, but I think these nurses like me. They do an awful lot of winkin' around here."

Yep. He's back to being Dad. A chuckle escapes then a huge sigh, feeling the relief in my bones.

I sit down in the chair by my dad, holding his hand, with Liam standing behind me, hands gently rubbing my shoulders. These two are very important men in my life and it makes me happy that Dad has taken a liking to Liam. Liam reminds me of him in many ways. Kind, protective, honest to a fault, giving.

I can sense Dad is starting to feel tired when he sighs and

closes his eyes, even with us still in the room. Mom sits on his other side, eyelids heavy. She needs to get home to rest as well. Dad is doing okay, so I think I'll suggest taking her home so she can nap for a while.

My muscles clench and my eyes close when I hear *that* voice getting louder as he nears my dad's room. It's Daniel again, and I'm pissed that Mom lied to me. She said he wouldn't be here. Not that I wouldn't have come anyway, it's just that I had no time to mentally prepare myself for this. I need to get Liam out of here before Daniel opens his big mouth about the pregnancy.

"So, um...Dad, we've got to get going." I stand and reach over to kiss my dad's forehead, squeezing his hand. When he looks at me, I know he knows, and his tired eyes tell me he understands. He pulls me in a little closer, cupping my face with his strong, hands and whispers to me, "You're okay, princess. I worry about you, ya know, and I love you."

Tears threaten, but I won't let them fall. "I love you too, Daddy. We'll see you tomorrow, okay? Mom, can we take you home to rest? Sydnee can bring you back later."

"I'm fine right here. Sydnee and Daniel can take me home later tonight. We'll come back tomorrow to pick up the old grump here," she jokes.

"Go on and get home, the both of you. And you don't need to be back here tomorrow, Sarah. I know you've got school, and little kids can get antsy when their teacher isn't there." Dad laughs and shoos us away quickly. We try desperately to make our exit before Daniel gets here.

No such luck.

When Daniel and Sydnee walk into the room, the tension goes from zero to infinity almost instantly, and Liam's clenched jaw and tense muscles are *not* a good sign. I don't know what it says about me that I like how protective he is because for the last five years, I've never needed protection from anyone or anything. Now, it's just hot, and I'm suddenly glad we've both got the whole day off, although if I don't get Liam out of here before they both open the flood-gates of sharing my past, I won't have to worry about him protecting me again.

We brush past the two of them out into the corridor. Unfortunately, they follow.

"Sarah, we need to talk." Daniel's voice grates on my nerves like chalk squeaking down a chalkboard.

"No, we don't. Let it go. Both of you." Jesus, I can't get out of here quick enough. I drop Liam's hand and take off toward the elevators, both Daniel and Liam on my heels.

"Sarah, wait." Liam catches up and his body stills behind me. He turns to Daniel but before he can make a move, I push past him, and I'm standing face-to-face with the man who broke my heart.

"I hate you." It was meant to be screamed, yet only came out in a hushed whisper.

"Did you tell him, Sarah? Did you tell him about the baby? And how you kept it from me? I mean, he is your new boy toy, right?"

"Shut the hell up, Daniel. You have *no* right." My stare is laser focused, while feelings of hatred and betrayal surface even after so many years have passed. To think I once loved this man is laughable considering the treatment I'm getting now. Liam had to have heard Daniel's questions. I can only hope and pray he understands why I didn't tell him and why I kept this from everyone.

"I had a right to know about *my* baby, Sarah?"

His baby? He can't even be serious. Heat flushes through my body as my pulse speeds up, but I will not let him get the best of me this time. With my eyebrows drawn together, chin held high, my lips flatten before I speak.

"You lost that right, asshole, when you screwed my sister.

How long were you with her behind my back before I finally caught you?" I question, the sound of my voice reaching a volume it clearly shouldn't inside of a hospital. How dare he bring this up, here of all places, and play the victim no less. "You make me sick. You *both* make me sick. You deserve each other."

Storming the rest of the way down the hall, I take deep breaths, trying to calm myself before Liam catches up again. The elevator button light goes out, indicating the doors are about to open, and that can't happen soon enough because my stomach turns and churns as my mind goes back to the day I lost the baby. The antiseptic smell of this place throws me back to when I was here six years ago and begins to wreak havoc on my insides, causing me to rush into the ladies' room. What little bit of food I'd had so far today comes up just as I reach the toilet. My wrists hang limply over my knees as I bend at my waist, sweat beading on my forehead.

"Sarah." There's a knock on the bathroom door and I hear Liam calling me from the hallway. "Sarah, are you okay?"

When I don't answer right away, the door flies open and in walks Liam, eyes wide and questioning. They're not the soft, ocean blue I've seen before. They're dark and irritated. Clearly with me.

"Are you okay?"

"I'm fine. Just an upset stomach. I'm...I'm good." The cool water feels good on my face and I quickly grab a paper towel.

Liam begins pacing back and forth, his hands running through his beautiful blond hair. He curses twice, causing me to jump. "What the hell was that back there? What baby is Daniel talking about?"

"Liam, please. Let's just get home."

"Tell me now, Sarah."

Two hospital employees are chattering with each other as

they walk in the rest room. Their voices and movements stop as soon as they see us.

"We were just leaving. I was sick, but I'm fine now. He was checking on me."

"Are you sure you're okay?" asks the older nurse, looking suspiciously at Liam.

"I'm fine. Just an upset stomach." I can feel Liam tense behind me, and then he gently reassures the women all is well as we make our way back into the hallway. God is the only one I have to thank when I see that Daniel and Sydnee are gone. The elevator doors open and we step inside. I can't even turn to face him. The silence is deafening.

"Is this the part of the story you left out when you told me about Daniel?" he asks in a low commanding voice, standing directly behind me, so close I can feel the rise and fall of his chest. I can't place this tone. Is it an angry one? I have no idea.

So, I say nothing. No words come. They don't come because the only thought in my mind is how Daniel has screwed me over a second time. I lost my baby and my sister because of him, and now I will lose Liam. If I could have told him on my own terms, in my own way, I may have had a chance. But I didn't, and now I'll have to face the consequences of that decision.

Seconds that feel like hours pass.

"I was pregnant with Daniel's baby when I was eighteen. Two days after I caught him with Sydnee in my bed, I lost the baby. A miscarriage. And now I..."

That's all I can say. Heavy tears stick to my eyelashes and when I finally blink, they fall to the floor.

Chapter Twenty

LIAM

Jesus. Sarah had been pregnant with Daniel's baby. The thought of another man touching her, being inside that sweet body, makes my head spin and my blood boil, but right now, my only concern is Sarah. And add to that, Daniel slept with her sister before he knew about the baby. What a shitstorm.

My Sarah.

She turns to face me, and the first thing I notice is her empty, sad green eyes staring at me, waiting to see what I will say, waiting for me to leave. She doesn't have to say a word for me to know that's what she's thinking. Slowly, my hand cups her the softness of her cheek, reddened by tears.

"Baby, I'm so sorry. I am so sorry. Why didn't you tell me?"

"And say what? I was a pregnant teenager, a statistic, knocked up by the boy who screwed my sister in my own bed?"

"Well, not exactly in those words. You know you did nothing wrong, don't you?"

She looks at me, seemingly confused at my response, not expecting it.

"You...you're not mad at me?"

"Why would you think I'd be mad? Babe, first of all, that was years ago, you were a teenager. Secondly, you didn't get pregnant on purpose. I'm sure, with the situation being what it was, you were under a tremendous amount of stress. I understand that."

"You do?"

"Sarah, if you think the miscarriage was your fault, it wasn't. You did nothing wrong. Is that why you didn't tell anyone...you thought it was your fault?"

She nods her head, and my heart absolutely breaks for this headstrong, determined woman who is falling apart right in front of me. For years, she's kept this secret inside, always believing she was to blame. Daniel is already at the top of my shit list, but this, blaming her for losing the baby, is beyond outrageous.

The doors to the elevator open and I hold onto Sarah, keeping her at my side. She is silent, except for the hitches in her breath as she fights off more tears. Never in a million years did I expect this, and it upsets me a bit she didn't think I would stick around if I found out. It totally explains the one-night stands. She doesn't allow men to get close for a reason and today I found out exactly why.

We walk together out of the hospital into the stillness of the early evening air. The sun is setting, making way for the stars to brighten up the night sky. We make our way through the busy parking lot to my car while I keep my arm around her waist as she pulls her jacket tighter around her for warmth, or maybe for security. Either way, I hold on to her.

Before I put the car in gear to pull out of the lot, I turn to Sarah. I need to say this to her and I pray to God she believes me. She may have avoided relationships in the past, but that shit stops today.

"Baby, I know right now you are spent. I can see the tiredness in your eyes. But please believe me when I say that this changes nothing. It doesn't change the way I feel about you, and it sure as hell doesn't change how I see you. You're still the most stunning, most caring, stubborn woman I've ever met. Carrying that shit around with you all these years has you believing things that aren't true. I am *not* him. I will *not* leave you. Ever. I love you, Sarah."

Slowly, her eyes find mine, and those heavy lashed lids blink slowly as if she's processing what I'm saying.

"You shouldn't. I can't give you what you want."

"What do you mean?"

Silence.

"Nothing. I'm just really tired. Can you please take me home?"

"I can. But I assure you, sweetheart, this conversation is not over. You are not pulling away from me, because I won't let you. Not now that I finally have you."

Chapter Twenty-One

SARAH

He doesn't understand. Last night, on our way home, he was quiet, giving me time, and I appreciated that. But I know what will happen. Eventually, he's going to want a family. He has such a capacity to love and as sure as the sun rises and sets every day, I know he will be an amazing father. Kids born into families like Liam's, close-knit families, most always want that same thing. He and his beautiful sisters will likely marry their beautiful significant others, and have an entire brood of beautiful kids running around, spending time together, celebrating holidays, going on vacations. That's what families like his do.

There are no pregnancies in the cards for me. Been there, done that, and have the scars to prove it. I don't think I could ever go through that kind of loss again. Never again will I allow myself to become pregnant and risk losing everything a second time. I barely survived the first nightmare. Liam will find out soon enough that I am not right for him long-term. I'm just a good *Miss Right Now*. Seems like that's all I've ever been.

"Sweetheart, you've got to talk to me at some point." The

frustration in his voice is evident as we sit together on the bench along the river while the sun sinks low, taking the warmth of the day with it. Liam picked me up for a quick dinner when I arrived home from school, and now here we are.

"I don't know what else you want me to say, Liam. I told you the entire sordid story on the way home from the hospital yesterday. There's nothing else. I got pregnant purely by accident, lost the baby, lost Daniel-which turned out to be a good thing-lost my sister, who no longer has a backbone to stand up to that asshole as evidenced by her behavior at the hospital, and basically lost my family because God forbid anyone do or say anything to upset Sydnee." Anger and sadness are fighting their way into my heart, trying to steal another piece of me. Like they haven't taken enough already.

"You told me at the hospital you couldn't give me what I want, and I'd like to know what it is *you* think I want. Clearly, you're not me, so how you have access to that information is somewhat of a mystery. Perhaps you can fill me in."

"Don't patronize, Liam." I shoot him a glare and hope the angrier he gets, the easier it'll be for me to break things off.

"Sweetheart, that's not patronizing. I'm trying like hell to figure all this out and for the life of me I can't understand how you think you know what it is that I want. Granted, we've been friends a while, and then we took that relationship a step further. But quite honestly, I haven't a clue as to what you think I want that you can't give me. I love you. You are everything to me."

I continue to stare straight ahead so I don't have to see the look on Liam's face. My voice breaks, my chin trembles and I feel the emptiness in my chest. The emptiness that remains from the miscarriage so many years ago. I've tried like hell to avoid this discussion with him, hoping to just shove it on the back burner for a while, enjoy what little time I have with him. But it looks like I've no other choice.

Swallowing down a gulp of air, I take a deep breath and ready myself for the conversation. My gaze shifts to Liam and I wish to God there was something I could do to change the path my life has taken. He is without a doubt the most wonderful man I've ever met and to have to tell him I don't want to have children has my stomach coiled tighter than a knot on a rope swing.

"The pain I felt the day I miscarried was unlike any other pain I've ever felt. Physically or otherwise." I half chuckle and shake my head, thinking back to the day when I thought losing Daniel was the worst possible feeling ever. "I wasn't dealing with Sydnee and Daniel's betrayal well, and the stress was too much for me to handle and I lost the baby. Some days, it seems like yesterday and others, it seems like a lifetime ago. But what I do know is that I will never put myself in that situation again."

Liam's eyes close, and his lips pinch together as he draws a deep breath then speaks through clenched teeth.

"I don't know what you want me to say to you, Sarah. I've told you repeatedly that I am nothing like that asshole. I. Am. Not. Daniel." The muscles in his neck are corded, and he is holding in that anger better than I ever would have. "I would never do anything so self-centered or selfish like that to you. Ever. When are you going to believe me?"

"It's not just that, Liam. I believe you when you say those things. I know you are not Daniel and you've proved that repeatedly. I feel so much more with you than I ever felt with him, and that's what makes this so hard."

"What? What's so hard, baby?!"

"I don't want to get pregnant, Liam. Ever. I won't go through that again." I didn't mean for it to come out quite so blunt. Now I feel half sick.

He stills suddenly, his head flinching back slightly.

"And I know how amazing your family is and how you'll want your life to be like that, with kids and all. I can't give you that. I won't put myself in the position to feel that kind of pain ever again." I take his hand in mine, wishing I could figure out a way to change all this, but it is what it is. "Please understand that I would do anything to change how I feel, but that ship's long since sailed. After the miscarriage, I vowed never again."

My hand is released from Liam's as he gets up and begins to pace in front of me. He massages the back of his neck and looks at me in surprise.

"That's it?"

Figuratively speaking, if my eyes could shoot daggers right now, Liam Reynolds' balls just might be my target. I am pissed.

"What the hell do you mean, *that's it*? You've got about two minutes to explain the shit out of what you just said before I walk."

He makes his way back to the bench, his hand caressing the side of my face. I flinch at his touch but he smiles and shakes his head. God, he's such a shit.

"Sweetheart, my God, you're amazing. I'm not making light of the situation, believe me. I guess *that's it* probably wasn't the best choice of words. What I meant was, is it babies that you think I want and you can't give me?"

"Well, yeah," my words fumbling just a bit. "You'll want your own family, your own kids."

"Who told you that? Do all couples have kids of their own, because I know of several who have chosen not to have kids, for one reason or another. I know two couples in my old neighborhood who adopted kids, which is a very admirable thing to do, by the way. Take a child who is no blood relation at all and give him a family." Without warning, he pulls me onto his lap, and I quickly look around to be sure we don't have an audience. "Honey, I appreciate that you think you're doing what's best for me, but don't. Don't assume to know what it is that I want before you even so much as ask."

"But, you do want kids, don't you? I mean..."

"I don't even know the answer to that. I've not thought too much about it, I suppose. But what I can tell you for certain is that if this works out between me and you, and I pray to God it does, if you and I decide we want kids, there are other ways to have them besides the traditional one. You not wanting to bear your own children is not a game changer for me. At all. Not even fucking close."

The softness in his voice and the hint of his sexy smile eases the tension in my muscles.

"But I thought-"

"Obviously you've been giving this too much thought," he interrupts. "We can talk about it, Sarah. That's what people do. Talk. Have a conversation. I know, over the past years, you've not wanted to be involved in any kind of relationship where talking was truly necessary. I get that...I understand why. But that ends now. Today."

His lips inch closer and closer to mine as his hands rub up and down my back. He hovers there for a heartbeat, or maybe ten, while one hand glides along my arm, across my shoulder and up to my neck, his thumb feeling the pulse in my vein. It's racing. He is so close that the heady scent of cologne and man mixed together makes me yearn for his lips on mine.

"Please tell me you understand."

I do. I do understand, but I sit here in silence, fighting the insecurities that have taken up space for far too long in my mind. I need to let them go, no longer giving them a voice. It's my time now.

"Yes." My voice cracks with emotion. "Completely."

"One of these days, you'll see yourself through my eyes. You'll see a magnificent woman who deserves to love and be loved. And who deserves someone who will give her the moon. I am that man, Sarah. I will be that man for you."

Chapter Twenty-Two

I've driven Sarah to see her dad a few times this week and she's thrilled at how well he is doing. He's resting, just as he was told, and not putting up too much of a fuss. Truthfully, I think he likes being waited on. He's a hardworking man, no doubt, but a little time off has done him a world of good. He and Mrs. Witten take slow walks around the neighborhood each day, so he's finally had the chance to get out and get fresh air.

Thankfully, we're able to visit at times where we can avoid Daniel and Sydnee. Only once since we've been there has Sarah seen Londyn, and I know she misses that little girl. She got to spend some quality time with her, doing hair and putting some make up on Little Londyn. That girl is a spitfire, kinda like Sarah, and I think she sees a lot of herself in her niece.

What's worrying me though, is Sarah. Even though we're talking and opening up more, and learning more intimate things about each other, I still feel like she's waiting for the other shoe to drop and it hasn't allowed her to let go and just be. She's not heard a peep from Daniel or her sister all week, and I know it's been on her mind. Can't say I blame her, though. This shitstorm is far from over if Daniel's behavior at the hospital last week was any indication. And her sister? Jesus, she just stood by and let Daniel have at Sarah. That guy has issues, and if I were a betting man, I'd offer up the farm and say Sydnee is just an emotional punching bag for him.

But for tonight, Sarah and I are headed to the pub. Business at Sam's has continued to pick up since the remodel. We've managed to get Samantha moved into the bar manager position and she decided on hiring two new bartenders and a new server. Once Tira, one of our servers, finally quit, we realized how very little she did around here, except for pissing everyone off. She single-handedly damn near ruined Zane and Raina's relationship, so no one was too keen on her sticking around anyway. Our new server, Dylan, has been working out well. The women seem to love him anyway. Occasionally, I see the sultry looks they give him, and I hear mumblings like, *he's so damn hot*, and *I'd love to serve him* getting thrown around, so he is a definite asset to the business. For some reason, Cole isn't a fan, and I think I can guess why.

I drag Cole away from the bar where he is deep in conversation with Samantha, even though she doesn't seem too hell-bent on listening to him. The rolling of the eyes and shaking of the head is a good indication she's had enough of his bullshit for one night.

"There is no way in hell she doesn't think I'm sexy. I mean, look at all this. I'm like crack to every woman I meet, Liam. They can't get enough. I think she's immune to my charm. Maybe she's a real-life witch because I'm the most charming guy I know."

"Or maybe she just sees you as too much work, too much drama."

"Drama? I'm the least dramatic person I know."

I wonder if he even hears himself sometimes. It's like talking to a twelve-year-old.

"For reals, man. *She's* the one. She's all up in my business, telling me I'm a man-whore, and I just tell her..."

Cole drones on and on, insisting he doesn't feed into the drama, as we make our way to the stage to start playing. Looking out, I see Sarah sitting at our table. We've spent nearly every evening together this week, doing a lot of talking and a shit ton of love making, all fire and passion. It's the one time where she can forget and get lost in the moment. Where she can let down her guard and her insecurities, and just be.

Our first song tonight I dedicate to her, and she blushes a beautiful pink when I announce it. "Kiss Me Slowly" by Parachute is a song I've always loved, and it's as though the lyrics were written for Sarah. I make eye contact with her, and hold on to her gaze as I sing, meaning each and every word.

"So, "Kiss Me Slowly," huh?" she asks when I pull up my seat beside her during our break.

"Absolutely, baby," I say as I pull her from her seat to sit down on my lap. I need her close. Without skipping a beat, she wraps her arms around me and she indeed does kiss me. Very slowly. It totally sucks that I've got one more set to play and a bar to close tonight, otherwise she'd be in my bed and we'd be not only kissing, but making love slowly.

"Hmmm. I like it," she whispers.

"I've got to stay here and close up in another hour. Once everyone leaves this place, you're mine."

"Right here in the bar?" Her eyes open wide and she looks around, trying to gauge how this is all going to play out.

"Right here in the bar. You got a problem with that?"

"Oh, no problem. I just don't...I don't want...an audience."

"Not on your life. Your sweet little body is for me, and only me. And I can't wait till I get to hoist it up on that bar right over there and have a little taste of my favorite snack," I whisper in her ear, running my hands up and down her thigh.

"Mmmm...can we close early if I kick everyone out?" she whispers, her head leaned back on my shoulder, hips grinding down on my dick.

"Baby, you've got to the count of five to stop grinding into me. I've got one more set to play and I can't do it hard as steel. Plus, Cole gets a little jealous. When we're on stage, he wants me all to himself. He's selfish that way," I say, laughing.

She giggles along with me, and then stills her hips. My body instantly misses her movement.

"We'll cut out a bit early and get this place tended to, and then it's me and you and a date at the bar, yeah?"

A very snarky grin makes its way to Sarah's face, and damn if she hasn't crawled into my heart and set up camp there. She makes me crave her like I've never craved another woman in my entire life.

THE LAST SET DRAGS ON, and I know it has everything to do with the fact that I have a *date* with Sarah *on* the bar once this place empties out. Soon enough, we're on our last song of the night and the crowd begins to thin out. Within the next thirty minutes, the bartenders, servers, Cole, and I work to get the place in order, close everything down, and then everyone heads out after another busy night.

"Let's go, Sammy! Get your *ass* in gear, babe!" Cole yells out, and judging by the scowl on Samantha's face, she's none too impressed.

"*Kiss* my ass, babe! It's Sam, not Sammy!" she yells back, pushing open the door with force and walking out without Cole.

"She just doesn't get it, does she?" he asks to no one in particular, shaking his head, as he follows her like a lost puppy out the door.

"That right there is gonna get interesting," I whisper to Sarah, then yell out to Cole. "Hey! Lock the door on your way out, *Casanova*."

Cole turns, giving me a middle finger salute. "Clean up your mess on the bar when you're finished, *asshole*. People eat and drink there, ya know."

Sarah looks at me, head tilted, lips pursed.

"What? I didn't say a thing. Can we please not think anymore about Cole right now. I'm losing my mojo here, babe, and I'm trying like hell to break in this new bar top with you."

Leaning back against the bar, I pull her between my legs, her hands running up and down my chest, heating skin she's not even touching. She pulls my shirt over my head and carelessly drops it on the floor. A seductive smile spreads across her face and she breathes deep, and winking flirtatiously. Her dress is lifted up over her head in one fell swoop, leaving nothing but a black lace bra and panties covering her...the barrier between paradise and me. In a matter of seconds, I grab her under her arms and lift her so her ass is perched on the edge of the clean, shiny bar, her legs spread wide, just waiting for me to get my fill.

It's only a matter of seconds before Sarah is divested of her bra and panties, all while I kiss her senseless. My tongue licks lazily along her stomach and down to what I call the promised land, making her squirm, where I lick and suck and devour her until her body is thrashing in the midst of a powerful orgasm.

The faint trace of stubble on my jaw leaves red scratches on the inside of Sarah's thighs, but it only fills me with pride. Kinda like a caveman, marking my woman, which makes me laugh.

It doesn't take long for her to reach for me, pulling me toward her, rubbing and grinding up against me, causing all the blood in my body to pool south, making my already hard cock feel like fucking cement. She moves her hips in circles, searching for more, and I can no longer wait to be inside her.

I line myself up with her wet opening and push right into paradise. This isn't slow and soft lovemaking. This is passion and heat and fire. My thrusts are fast-paced, rocking Sarah back and forth on the bar top so forcefully, she grabs hold of the rail and holds on.

"Shit, Sarah. You are so wet, so warm, baby. I can't get enough of you."

Her only responses are whimpers and moans. I've rendered her speechless.

Yep, it was that good.

Chapter Twenty-Three

LIAM

This is it. I have to have this conversation now, as much as I don't want to. Sarah's just gotten off the phone with her mom and thankfully Mr. Witten is doing remarkably well. Sarah had been working on schoolwork when her mom called, and I've been getting caught up on some paperwork from the bar I brought home to finish. Concentrating on these numbers is becoming increasingly difficult the more I think about what I'll say to her. With my laptop and a folder of papers put away for now, I walk to the sofa to sit by my girl, hoping for the best.

"You about finished?"

"Just finishing now. Help me get these papers in my bag and I'll put away my laptop."

Once everything is cleaned up, I grab a beer from the fridge and get a glass of wine for Sarah, sitting close to her, hoping to keep her grounded.

"Sweetheart, a few weeks ago when Roman and Tatum came to hear me play, Roman took some video of Cole and I playing some of our original stuff. He's a musician as well, and it so happens his father is a record executive. Roman showed his father the video and he would like Cole and I to go to Nashville to talk with a rep there. I haven't a clue what will happen in that meeting, or who all will be there. We're just going to hear what they have to say and what they may be interested in. It could turn out to be a wasted trip, for all I know."

Sarah is silent, but her body language is speaking volumes. I frame her face with my hands, leaning in to kiss her gently. Her body is tense and there's an uneasy look in her eyes. "You have to know I love what we're building here between us, and also with the bar. I'm not making any decisions about anything without you. Not sure how long we'll be there, but I suspect only a few days. As soon as I know, you'll know." My voice stays as calm as I can make it, hoping she'll clue in on that.

"Yeah. Um, that's great, Liam. I hope that works out for you. I know your music is important to you."

"You've become *more* important. I love you, remember?"

She's shifting on my lap, twiddling those fingers again and pulling at the hem in her shirt, which is her tell. She's nervous, I know it, because her voice cracked twice, and her eyes never once met mine. Looking uncertain, she withdraws her hand from mine and I instantly feel the loss of it. I put her on my lap on purpose because I could hold on to her better if she tried to get up to leave too quickly. She's finally settling into this committed relationship with me, but because of her past, I expected there would be a good chance she'd take off after hearing this news.

"I know you've got school, but I'd love for you to come with us."

"Liam, you know I can't take time off school. You said yourself you don't know how long you'll be there. I just can't go running off in the middle of the school year to Nashville, to see if my boy...I mean, to see if you're going to get some record deal. That's your dream anyway, not mine."

"My dream, Sarah, was always to become a songwriter. This meeting may lead to that, it may lead to some kind of record deal, or it may end up being nothing, which I'm inclined to believe the latter because cracking the music industry is not just having the talent. It's a lot of being in the right place at the right time and some good luck too. To be perfectly honest, Cole is the one who is counting most on a record deal. He's got bright lights and money and women on his mind right now, and not in that order. And honestly, if that is something he'd like to pursue, I would support him all the way. It doesn't mean that's what I have to do too. My other dream was to meet an amazing woman someday, and start planning a future. Right now, I can see that particular dream coming true."

"What do you want me to say, Liam? I'm happy for you. I really am. It's just..."

"That the timing sucks?" I question.

"Well, yeah, the timing sucks." The defeated sound in her quiet voice pierces my ears and I don't like it.

"Look, I'll call you every night, we'll Face-Time, or Skype, or whatever. It's just a couple days, I'd imagine. And you know what they say about absence and the heart?" I try to tickle her and get her to lighten up some, and I know she's trying, it's just the smile is forced, not heartfelt. "Sarah, I am not leaving you. I'm coming back because this right here," I say, wiggling my finger between the two of us, "this is the real deal, and now that you're finally mine, don't even think for one minute that I would ever give this up. We will make it work. I promise."

For the first time since we started this conversation, Sarah smiles. A genuine smile, not a *smile-because-that's-what-I-should-do* smile. I breathe a sigh of relief and pull her closer to me, situating her legs so she's straddling my lap. My lips hover over hers briefly.

"You're amazing, you know that?"

"Eh...I've heard that a time or two," she jokes.

"Oh, you have, have you? Well, let's see how amazing you really are then." My tongue sneaks out to lick the perimeter of her luscious lips.

"Liam, are you propositioning me?"

"You call it whatever you want to call it." My lips meet hers again and in a few short moments, we're lost in each other for the second time today.

Sarah and I leave to go to the Winter Carnival her school is hosting tonight. She's signed up to work the cotton candy station and when she told me that, my mind conjured up all sorts of images of Sarah covered in sticky sweetness and my tongue licking off all that goodness.

This, however, is an elementary school function, so I need to keep the X-rated version of the cotton candy station in the back of my mind.

Raina coerced Zane into helping, and I'm not exactly sure how she did it, but she roped Cole into working this event too, and I, for one, can't wait to watch him in action. He'll fit right in with the ten-year-olds. God help us all, he's running the bouncy house. He asked Sam to come with him, but she's having none of what he's offering right now. Besides, she's back at the bar, large and in charge, for the night. With the three of us here, at least one manager had to stay back and keep the place running.

We all arrive at the school at the same time and walk in together, finding our stations and setting up. Before we even hit the main entrance, Sarah had to remind Cole three times this was a family event and to leave the sailor language at the door. And she had to do that when Cole announced, "Fuck, let's do this," as we opened the school doors.

These were the kinds of events I always looked forward to as a kid. We'd get all hyped up on sugary treats then head home to crash, our asses dragging the next morning as we tried to pull ourselves out of bed for the school day.

"So, this carnival thing. Do you get lots of kids?" I ask Sarah.

"Oh, we definitely do. They've been looking forward to it for weeks now. We've read carnival stories and did carnival math, and learned about how spinning sugar turns into cotton candy in science, so I think we've done a great job turning this into a learning experience too."

One of the first things I noticed about Sarah in this environment, with her fellow teachers and all the kids, is how relaxed she is. This place, these kids, they take her mind off all the bullshit she's been through and allow her to shine. To do what she does best.

"Miss Witten! Miss Witten!"

Sarah braces herself for a flailing seven-year-old approaching at a speed that may possibly reach Mach 10.

"I knowed you'd be here. I jus' knowed it!" The little girl bounces up and down on her toes, grabbing Sarah around the waist.

"Alyssa, sweetie, I told you all week I'd be here, remember?"

"Oh, I remember, I really do, I think I jus' forgot, can I have some cotton candy?" There are no breaks in her sentences, no pauses, not one breath taken. It all comes barreling out at once. This little one's smile lights up the entire place and she holds on to Sarah like she's Santa Claus or something.

"Well, do you have the ticket I gave you?"

"Sure do, here ya go. Who's this guy?" the little one asks, pointing straight at me.

"Alyssa, this is Liam. Liam, this is Alyssa."

Once I stop my head from spinning after that brief but confusing conversation, I kneel down, shaking Alyssa's hand.

"Nice to meet you, Alyssa. That's a pretty name."

"Yep. You gonna marry Miss Witten?"

Sarah's lips pull into a tight line, and she tries quite hard to stifle a grin, dropping her head so I don't see the redness appear on her face.

"Alyssa, Liam and I are good friends."

"Okay. Miss Witten, I have to go to the bouncy house now, I have a ticket for that too."

"Hey Alyssa, make sure you talk to the man who is working the bouncy house tonight. His name is Cole. He loves talking. He talks a lot, so be sure to stay there a while, okay?"

"Okay, Li...um...Li. Okay, just Li, that's it," she says, struggling to remember my name.

I can't help but howl with laughter as soon as little Alyssa leaves to find the bouncy house. I can see why Sarah is so taken with these kids. It's a wonderful age. It makes me sad to think of all she will be missing by not being a mother, either to her own, or to a foster or adopted child. I try to understand why she's scared. She was so young when she miscarried, though, and I think if she would talk to someone about it, get her feelings and insecurities about another pregnancy out in the open, it may just help her see that trying to have another baby someday may just be a risk worth taking.

My mind drifts to a time when she would be pregnant with my child. God, I can just see her now. A beautiful round belly, soft curves. As good as she is with these kids, she would be the most nurturing and caring mom, I can feel it. I just know. And she'd deliver that baby like a champ. Oh, she'd scream at me, no doubt. That's a given. I smile at the sound of my stubborn girl giving me hell for knocking her up. "Liam!" she'd yell over and over, squeezing my hand as she delivers our baby.

"Liam!" It sounds so real, like I really hear her voice.

"Hey, Liam!" And when I turn, there she is, snapping her fingers in my face, frustration on hers. "You gonna stand there all day with your head in the clouds or are you gonna help me make cotton candy?"

"Shi...I mean, shoot. Sorry about that. Lost in thought."

"I'll say. Now get me the good stuff and let's get these kids all sugared up."

The night passes quickly, most likely due to the fact that we made upwards of seven hundred pounds of cotton candy. And I don't think that's an exaggeration. I'm covered in this shit. Sarah has little pieces of blue and pink strewn through her hair, yet she's never looked more beautiful to me.

"Jesus, these kids have too much energy. Why do kids have all this energy and grown-ups have none? Seems a bit lopsided if you ask me," Zane groans as he and Raina walk up to the cotton candy machine Sarah and I are cleaning.

"Don't pick on the kids, Zane. They're probably on a sugar high from all the cotton candy Sarah and Liam fed them."

"No kid of mine will ever touch that shit. I guarantee you that."

"Well, baby, I guess we'll find out soon enough." Raina walks closer to Zane, reaching for his hand. Every head turns to Raina as one lonely tear falls down her face, and when she smiles at Zane, he gets it. It sinks in. He's gonna be a father.

"You m–me–mean..." Zane stutters.

"Yes, I do. I'm pregnant."

The loudest scream that's ever been recorded on this planet comes out of Zane's mouth. He picks up Raina, twirls her around, probably throwing her into a bout of vertigo. Jesus, she's pregnant and he's spinning her around like a wind-up top.

"Oh, my God, baby, really? Shit, I shouldn't spin you around, should I? I'm sorry. You're really pregnant?"

"Really, really. Eight weeks along."

"Oh, Raina, I'm so happy for you. I knew Zane had those super sperm." Sarah pushes Zane out of the way and leans in to give Raina a hug, rubbing her hand up and down Raina's back.

Everyone laughs at Sarah's comment and gathers around to congratulate the happy couple on their news. And when I turn to look at Sarah, what *I* see is not what everyone else sees. Everyone else sees a smile, sees her clapping along with the group. I see profound sadness. The tears building in her eyes aren't happy ones, although she'll tell you they are. The slump in her shoulders is just because she's tired, she'll tell you. When she drops her head, she'll say she's thinking about how excited she is for Raina, and how she's wondering if it'll be a boy or girl. Yeah, she'll put on a front to make everyone else believe she couldn't be happier, because no one else but me, and of course her family and shithead Daniel, knows she miscarried at eighteen. If Raina knew this, she'd never have announced her pregnancy like she just did.

The mask of happiness that's slid down over Sarah's face? It's just that. A mask. Fake. And I wonder if I'll be able to pull it off, or if we're back to square one.

I take Sarah's hand, squeezing it in a show of support.

"All I can say is I'm glad I don't have that shit to worry about," Cole interrupts. "After tonight, I might just wrap my dick in bubble wrap so I don't have to worry about kids. Like ever. These little rug-rats wouldn't leave me alone. And this little girl, Lyssi or Lyssa or something, Jesus, she talked my ear off all night."

"You do realize they're drawn to you because you act their age, you know. I mean you basically have the same mental capacity."

"Raina, that's the meanest thing you've ever said to me. You're a teacher, babe, so I think you really need to start working on using your nice words."

"Awww...didn't mean to hurt your feelings, big guy," she shoots right back.

"Keep up the sarcasm, go ahead," he says with fake annoyance. "I can take it. I'm leaving now, so I can go home and order some bubble wrap, or at the very least, double strength condoms. Lock down this shit now."

We're all walking out the door of the school and Sarah and I break off toward my car. I can tell Sarah's mind is a mile away. As we reach the car, I stop, pulling her to lean on me as I rest against the door.

"Babe, you look beautiful with cotton candy in your hair," I say, smiling. "And before you say a word, I mean that. You are beautiful." I pick the sticky little pieces of blue and pink out of her hair, dropping them to the ground.

"Baby colors," she whispers in a voice so low, it barely registers.

"What?"

"Pink and blue. Baby colors. The hospital had these little pink and blue blankets that the babies were wrapped up in. All the moms were holding their babies in pink and blue blankets. I didn't get to hold a pink and blue blanket, Liam."

"Oh God, sweetheart, I'm so sorry." With my hand around the back of her head, I draw her to me. She grabs my shirt and holds on, sobbing, hiccups and tears like I've never seen. My heart has never felt so broken for another human being in my life. "I love you, sweetheart. No matter what, I love you. Whatever you need for me to do to help you, I'll do it. I promise." That's all I can say. I just hold on to her, and let her break, knowing it will be me who puts her back together.

Her eyes, rimmed red, find mine, and through the sadness, there's something else there I can't quite place.

"Liam, I..." she hesitates.

"Yeah, baby?"

She raises up on her toes, her lips nearly touching mine. When her head tilts downward, I take the opportunity to rest my lips on her forehead. Damn, if she doesn't taste like cotton candy, all sugary and sweet.

"I love you too," she all but whispers into my shirt, clinging to me like a life raft.

Finally.

Because of the position we're in right now, I'll let it go this time, but next time she says those words to me, we'll be face-to-face, eye to eye, so I can finally see what Sarah looks like when she's in love.

Chapter Twenty-Four

SARAH

I said it. I told Liam I loved him. Do I regret that? Absolutely not.

I can't imagine how it's possible there is a man out there like Liam. He's different than any other man I've ever met. He's a rare breed, he and Zane. Raina caught herself a good man, and it appears I've done the same. Instead of running from me when I told him about being pregnant as a teenager, he pulled me closer and said he understood. He consoled and listened to me more so than my mom ever did.

She was in such a hurry to sweep it all under the rug, so we could all just go back to being the big happy family we were before. That didn't happen. Didn't even come close. Appearances mean a lot to her, so the less drama with the whole Daniel and Sydnee affair, the better. The entire mess couldn't be over fast enough in her eyes.

With Liam, I found comfort and understanding. I found him willing to listen. Not just hear my words, but take them in, process them, and use what I was feeling to support me in every way possible, physically and emotionally.

So, yep, I do love him. Am I nervous? Damn straight, I

am. I locked my heart down tight after Daniel. Cemented the hell out of it so no one would get in. Swore I'd never fall in love again.

But Liam is different. He came along with a damn chisel and took it upon himself to pick apart the wall bit by bit, chunk by chunk, until he finally had access to my heart, and when he had it, he took full advantage, so much so that nothing I could do would keep me from falling for him.

It's been a week since the parking lot incident, as I refer to it, where I pretty much lost it when I found out Raina was pregnant. I wasn't disillusioned enough to think it would never happen, it just caught me completely off guard. My mind immediately went back to the night at the hospital, the doctors and nurses, everyone around consoling me after I'd learned I'd miscarried. The sterile, cold smell, the hustling and bustling of the ER staff, the crying of a child and his mother trying to comfort those cries. All of it became real to me again, and put me right back to that moment in time. Liam wasn't there with me when I went through that nightmare the first time around, but he was there for me when the memories of that night resurfaced. And once again, his presence had a calming effect on me. I don't know how he does it.

Right now, we're at Liam's, working to get things packed for his trip to Nashville with Cole, and to say that also makes me nervous is an understatement. He's leaving for a few days, but I keep reminding myself he's not leaving me. He is *not* Daniel.

What does concern me most is what may happen if he and Cole are offered some kind of recording contract, where that puts us. Because Nashville is a big no. I love living in a small town and I've grown to feel comfortable here, with the people, the community, and the parents and kids here.

"I can't imagine the energy it takes to do that much thinking."

"Liam, inside my head is a place that no one but me belongs. It gets scary in there, trust me."

Liam chuckles, taking my hand, and pulls me in close.

"You remember everything I told you about this trip? It's nothing more than a conversation. That's all."

"I know. Believe me, I've told myself that very thing over and over again. It's on replay in my mind. It's what comes after the conversation that I'm having a hard time with."

"Well, since we don't know exactly what will happen after the conversation, let's just put that aside for now until we know for sure, yeah?"

"I can try. I just want you to know something before you go."

"And what's that?" Liam asks, running his hand up under my shirt, grazing the hook of my bra then tugging it free.

"You're not listening," I whisper, smiling when his lips land on the sensitive skin behind my ear.

"Mmm...you smell so good, baby. Taste so good. Can we have this conversation in about an hour or so?" My shirt is yanked up over my head, and upon seeing the desire filling Liam's eyes, immediately I decide that, yes, we can table this conversation for later.

"Oh, God," I moan, feeling his hands gliding down my back-side, into my leggings and panties, guiding them down so I can quickly step out of them. He kisses his way back up my legs, stopping when he hits the juncture of my thighs, kissing me there so intimately, while his fingertips lightly caress my lower back and ass.

Liam stands at the same time I pull my bra the rest of the way off which leaves me there in front of Liam, completely naked and exposed. All the while, he's fully-clothed in his worn jeans that hang low on his hips and his casual black Henley.

"This will never do," I say, moving to rid him of his shirt. He reaches up over his head, pulling it off as my hands skate along his sexy, toned abs, and down along the elastic of his boxer briefs that peek just above the waistband of his jeans.

"When you run those fingertips of yours along my skin, it's like fire, Sarah. Jesus, I can't get enough of you."

Liam makes short work of his jeans and boxer briefs then lifts me up, walks into his bedroom and gracefully lays me across his neatly made, king-size bed. He hovers over me, propped up on one arm while his other hand caresses my skin, from my fingertips to my shoulders and the back of my neck. I lean up, silently asking him to kiss me and he does. Kissing Liam is like nothing I've ever experienced. It's sensual and passionate, as if he's pouring out his feelings for me.

Soon, Liam's fingers are right at my center, softly moving circles. He's teasing me, causing me to rotate my hips around and back and forth, trying to find what I need.

"You are quite needy tonight, Miss Witten. Something you want?"

"Liam, you know exactly what I w–want," I stutter, as he rubs right over the spot where I need him most. "Oh, God. Stay there. Right there. If you move, so help me, I'm getting my vibrator and I'll finish it myself."

"Shit, Sarah. You got toys, baby?" Liam chuckles. "Damn. How did I not know this?"

"Liam, please don't stop."

"Not on your life," he responds seriously. "Come, Sarah. Come for me."

Only seconds pass, and I'm in the throes of an orgasm, my back arching, my legs shaking. I groan at the loss of his fingers, but soon feel his cock at my entrance, hard and ready.

"Eyes, Sarah. Let me see your eyes when I take you."

My eyes open at his command, and when he is finally and completely inside, he nearly collapses on top of me, his hands running through my hair, his lips covering mine in a wild, frenzied kiss. I allow my hands to run up and down along his smooth, muscular back, gripping his shoulders with every thrust, feeling his strength as he all but consumes me, making me ache in the sweetest of ways. Making me needy as he whispers dirty words in my ear.

I can't tell you how long we make love. When I'm with Liam, there's no counting seconds or minutes or hours. We're not racing to the end because we're far too engaged in pleasuring each other. Time means nothing to either of us when we're this connected.

And now, both of us lay sated on Liam's bed, cuddled together, covered only by a sheet. His fingers twirl through the soft curls on my head as he lays there, humming a tune I know all too well...Eric Clapton. It's one of my favorites and I'm overcome with emotion as he sings. He continues humming the song, and soon my eyes are blinking slower and slower.

"Sleep, baby. I'll wake you before I leave."

"Good night, Liam."

Chapter Twenty-Five

LIAM

Watching Sarah sleep while I'm getting ready to head out is giving me time to do a tremendous amount of thinking. Just looking at her, how at peace she is, how content, gives me pause. That gorgeous, silky hair fanned across my pillow, her breasts barely covered by the sheet, and arms spread out wide to each side, she looks like every boy's wet dream come to life. There isn't a picture in a single nudie magazine that could even come close to this beauty.

The bed dips when I sit next to her and I laugh as she rolls to the side, the sheet pulled away, revealing those gorgeous tits.

Damn. Why do I have to leave right now?

"Baby?" I lean in and whisper, then kiss her softly on her forehead.

"Hmmm, yes..."

"That's what you said last night. About three times, as a matter of fact."

Her vivid green eyes open to find mine, and when she focuses her vision completely, she smiles. I know right then I want to wake up to this beauty, this amazing woman, every single day for the rest of my life.

"At least three. I'm thinking probably four, if I remember correctly."

"Or was it six?"

"Don't flatter yourself, Liam. You pulled four amazing orgasms out of me last night but, if I'm able to walk today, then you didn't do your job, stud."

I throw back my head in laughter, swatting her on the ass.

"Oh, I did my job. And thoroughly, I might add. I've gotta go, babe. I'm picking up Cole in fifteen. He's texted me three times already. Seven and a half hours in the car with him might just put me over the edge," I say, jokingly.

Sarah smiles hesitantly. She sits up in bed as I reach out to tuck a few strands of hair behind her ear, hoping my touch provides a sense of comfort for her. My fingers trail down her cheeks.

"I'll call every night. I promise. And just so you know, when I get back in town, you better not have made any plans at all for...I'm thinking, a minimum of three days straight. That's how much time I'm gonna need with you all to myself."

"Three days it is then. I miss you already."

"I love you, sweetheart. So much more than I think you even realize."

"I love you too, Liam. And I'll be okay. Don't worry about me."

"Not possible. There's a key on the stand by the door. It's yours...and I don't want it back."

"Liam..."

"Ever. I don't ever want it back."

Leaning in, I kiss my girl, brushing one lone tear from her cheek. "You make me so happy. See you soon, baby."

Turning to walk out the door, I stop for a brief moment.

Something doesn't feel right. I'm not sure what to call it...there's just a gut feeling I have right now. I shake it off, figuring it's just the thought of being away from Sarah for these next few days. That has to be it.

I close the front door gently, hoping Sarah's gone back to sleep for a while, then hop in the car, ready to pick up Cole and head to Nashville, the place I used to think held all my hopes and dreams. Now I believe all my hopes and dreams are right here in Hillsborough, and she's sleeping in my bed right now.

Chapter Twenty-Six

SARAH

True to his word, Liam has called me every night. He and Cole met with Roman's dad and with someone named Chrissie, which, to me, is a name that sounds way too juvenile and perky to be an important woman in the music business. But whatever. That's just me being a tad jealous that she's got his attention right now and not me.

He and Cole are thrilled that two of Nashville's hottest country stars want to record two of their original songs. The same two Roman had sent to his father and he passed along to this Chrissie. I have to admit, this option is the best I could have hoped for because that means Liam will hopefully be able to stay here, with me, and write his music for other artists. So, the dilemma of a long-distance relationship is likely solved. Being a songwriter was always the end goal for him anyway. Now Cole? That's another matter altogether. Liam said he was disappointed at first, as he was hoping for a recording contract, so he and Liam could release their own album, but he really began to come around to the idea of songwriting once they met with the two artists who wanted to record their music. And who knows, if Cole wants a record deal bad enough, he's stubborn enough to make it happen.

Sitting at home, I'm indulging in a glass of wine while I work on plans for school. I've talked to Liam already this evening, so I decide to pack up my teacher bags and use this time to relax and unwind after a long week with the kids.

A knock sounds at the door and I'm confused at first as to who that might be. Raina and Zane are home, I just talked to her. I've already visited Mom and Dad today. And Lord knows, I'd never step foot in Sydnee's house anymore.

I put my wine glass on the table and walk to the door. Looking out the side window, I see Daniel. My heart skips a beat and most definitely not in a good way. I open the door and start to ask him why he's here and what he wants; however, he decides to barge right into my house, along with the coolness of the night air, nearly knocking over the small stand where I keep my keys and umbrellas.

"What in the hell are you doing here?"

Daniel turns to face me and suddenly I'm afraid because this is not a look I've ever seen on his face before. He's clearly been drinking...the stench of alcohol is overpowering. His clothes are disheveled and his hair looks as though he hasn't combed it in weeks.

"What in the hell am I doing here? I'll tell you what I'm doing here. I wanna know why you didn't tell me about the baby. I had a right to know."

"Like hell you did. I came home from shopping that day, six years ago, wanting to see you and tell you I was pregnant. But what did I find? You and Sydnee, screwing around *on my bed*. I don't owe you a thing, Daniel. Not a damn thing."

"Oh, you most certainly do, sweetheart."

"I'm not your sweetheart, Daniel. Save that title for Sydnee. Remember her? Your *wife*? She's the one you chose."

"Do you have any idea what this has done to Sydnee and me? Jesus, she is so upset and mad." He's pacing back and forth, massaging his neck with his hand, obviously very irritated. "And it's your fucking fault!" he screams, picking up my wine glass and throwing it across the room. "She's worse than you."

His steps are subtle, but I can see him moving toward me, inch by inch. And when I look into those eyes, the ones I used to love, all I see is resentment and hate. They're black and they're angry. For the first time in my life, I'm afraid of him.

"You fucking ruined it all, you know. Hell, you probably got pregnant on purpose. Tried to trap me. Is that it? You knew you'd never be able to hold on to me, so you got pregnant? And you're so pathetic, you couldn't even hold on to the baby, now could you. You lost it. You lost my baby."

My fault.

I lost my baby.

I pull in a deep breath, fighting off the memories. My trembling voice cracks in fear as I try to warn him away from me. What did I ever see in this man? And how did he turn into this?

"Get out, Daniel. Just go home and I won't tell Sydnee you even came here."

"Fuck her. She drives me crazy, always so needy, always whining. She deserves the shit she gets." I hate the fact that little Londyn has to live in the same house with this monster. I'm afraid for her, and afraid for Sydnee now as well.

At a quick glance, I see my phone still on the counter, so I push Daniel in the center of his chest, knocking him off balance, then move quickly to grab it and take off down the hall, slamming and locking my bedroom door. Dialing as fast as I can, I connect to Raina.

"Raina, hurry. Please get Zane and hurry. Daniel is here." I scream when I hear him banging on the door to my room. "Shit!"

"Open this fucking door now! *Now*, Sarah!"

"Sarah, oh my God. Okay. Stay put, babe. We're on our way. I'm calling nine-one-one."

"Please hurry, Raina. Oh, God. Please hur–"

The phone drops out of my hands at the sound of Daniel's boots slamming into the door, causing me to panic. I try as best as I can to push the dresser in front of the door, but it's no use. It's too heavy. With one final blow, the door is busted open.

Oh my God. I've never seen evil until now.

"Daniel, don't do this. Daniel, please. You're drunk. You don't want to do this. Think of Londyn. She needs you, right? She needs her daddy." There's only so far I can back away before I hit the mattress on my bed.

"Where's your man tonight, Sarah? He leave you too? Huh?"

"He...he's on his way over ri–right now, so you should leave."

"Nah. I think I'll stay. Let him see how much trouble you cause. He'll figure out you're not worth it eventually. Didn't take me too long to figure out I was screwing the wrong sister."

Those wild eyes hyper-focus in on me, and now I'm not so sure he isn't strung out on some kind of drugs.

"Dan..." My voice cracks in fear. The overpowering scent of too much cologne and the smell of alcohol nauseates me. This isn't the Daniel I fell in love with. This is an entirely different man.

I don't even see him raise his hand to me, but I sure as hell feel it when an open palm smacks right across my cheek, causing me to lose my footing and fall to the floor. Pain explodes across my face again when he lands a second hit, then grabs my hair, dragging me up off the floor, slamming me on the bed.

"Daniel, stop!"

I brace myself for the next blow, trying to cover my face with my hands, to kick him away, which only aggravates him more. I scream out, then suddenly he's not there. He's being dragged away from me and when I look up, I see Zane locking both of Daniel's arms behind his back and hurling him against the wall.

"What the fuck, man. Let me go!" Daniel screams.

Zane eyebrows are drawn together, his eyes wide open and glaring. He says nothing but uses the strength of his body to hold Daniel there. Within seconds, I hear the sirens. Grabbing onto the pillow, I scoot myself back against the headboard of the bed, holding onto the side of my face and wincing in pain. The police officers enter my room, a couple minutes later, with Raina right behind them. She rushes over to my bed, grabbing hold of me, and not letting go.

"Get him the hell off me!" I hear Daniel screaming as the policeman reaches for his hands, cuffing his wrists behind his back. "Take it easy, man. Watch it."

"Oh my God, Sarah. Are you okay?"

"Ra-Raina. Raina, don't leave me." My voice comes out in a whisper, my hands still trembling in fear. "I...I..."

"Oh, sweetheart, we're here. Zane and I are here. They're taking Daniel now, okay. They're taking him away."

Raina holds me as we watch the officers wrestle Daniel out of my room, Zane on their heels, explaining my phone call and what he witnessed when he entered my room. Panic begins to set in again and I can't breathe. I'm struggling to breathe, taking quick breaths in and out. I need to stand. I need to get out of this room.

"Honey, you've got to calm down. You're hyperventilating. Just calm down. Slow breaths." Raina stands close behind me, her hands on my shoulders. "Come back over here and sit."

But I can't. I can't stop. Without warning, dizziness sets in, everything around me fading in and out of focus, and within minutes, my world goes black.

Chapter Twenty-Seven

SARAH

"Sarah," I hear my best friend's voice whispering.

"Raina?"

"Jesus, you scared the shit out of me. Are you okay, sweetie?"

"God, my face hurts."

"You were hyperventilating and passed out. You've only been out a minute, though. Are you sure you're okay?"

Panic sets in once again, remembering Daniel. Where is he? I shoot straight up but grab my head immediately when the pain races up the side of my face to the top of my head.

"Where is he? Where's Daniel?" I look around frantically.

"Slow down, Sarah. He's gone. He's being taken to the police station. Two officers are still here, and they'd like to talk to you if you think you're okay."

One of the officers steps forward, kneeling down so we're eye to eye. It's comforting.

"Miss Witten, we'd like to take a statement, if you're up to it. We'd need specific information about what happened before your friends arrived. Can you answer some questions for us?"

"He's gone?"

"Yes, ma'am, he's gone. Down to the station."

"Okay. Okay. I can do that."

"Let's go out to your living room where you can sit, get a drink maybe. Take a couple minutes to make sure you're okay." The officer leads us out of my bedroom and we both sit at the small dining table near the kitchen. Raina pulls a water from the fridge, handing it to me, while Zane wraps an ice pack in a thin towel for my face. Jesus, it still stings.

"Zane and I will be in the living room while you talk to the officer, okay?"

"Yeah. I'm good. I'm all right."

The officer asks a few questions and writes down as much information as I can give him. It's when he gets to *why* Daniel attacked me that I begin to break down all over again. How many more times will I have to relive the night I lost my baby?

Tears form in my eyes as I recount the last days of our relationship and how I never told him I was pregnant but lost the baby. I tell him my mother told Daniel and my sister about the miscarriage, and about how angry he was when he found out.

"Okay, Miss Witten. I think that's all for tonight. If we have any other questions or need any more information, we'll be in touch. You get some rest. We've got it from here."

"Thank you," I whisper. "Thank you for helping me."

The officer smiles a sad smile and reminds me to go to the hospital to get checked over if I feel like I need to. He leaves through the front door and as I close it behind him, I turn, letting my back fall against it, sliding to the floor in tears.

Before I can make a move to get up, Zane is picking me up off the floor and taking me to the sofa to sit. Raina comes to sit beside me, putting her arm around my shoulder and pulling me close. I hear Zane walking toward my bedroom where I assume he's going to tend to the broken-down door.

"Honey, let's get a bag packed for you and you can come to stay with Zane and me at my apartment. We've got plenty of room."

"Are you sure? I mean…"

"Sarah, there's plenty of room. And we can talk if you want. I heard the story you told the officer. Honey, I had no idea." Tears begin to fall from her eyes and we just sit there, her wrapping me in a hug, being the most supportive best friend I've ever had.

"The door is fixed as best I can for now. I can hit the hardware store tomorrow and take care of it. We'll get her a new door."

"Thanks, love. Let's help her get some clothes and get her over to our place," Raina replies.

I grab a bag from the closet, throwing in PJ's and a change of clothes for tomorrow. In the bathroom, I gather some things I know I'll need, and just as I'm about to toss them in my small make-up bag, I catch my reflection in the mirror and gasp. Bruises are already forming on my cheek from being Daniel's punching bag. My hand covers my mouth as I fight away more tears.

Another nightmare.

Another reason why I should just be alone.

Chapter Twenty-Eight

LIAM

O ur bags are packed and we're ready to head out, back to Hillsborough, in the morning. It's been a long day of meetings with executives, lawyers, and a shit ton of other people in this business and I'm exhausted. I'll be glad to sleep in my own bed tomorrow night and I'll be even happier to see Sarah. I've missed her more than I thought I would. Interestingly enough, Cole has mentioned he'll be glad to get back as well. He says it's so he can check on how Samantha is doing as the new bar manager. I said nothing in return. I'll just let him think that's the reason, but I know better. He can't admit how into her he really is, and it makes me laugh.

My cell phone buzzes and I grab it to answer the call. It's Zane.

"Hey, man. What's up?"

"You still planning on coming home tomorrow?" he asks, which is weird. He knows this.

"Yeah. Sure. Leaving right after breakfast."

"Okay. Good." His voice sounds way off. Something's wrong.

"Zane, what's going on?"

"We'll see you when you get back. It's okay."

"No, it's not okay. What's wrong?"

"Okay, listen. Everyone's okay. She's good. But it's Sarah. Daniel paid her a little visit tonight and let's just say, he ended up at the police station after it was all over."

"Zane, tell me right the hell now what happened." My breathing picks up, and I'm wondering what happened to cause Daniel to end up at the police station. "What the hell did he do?"

"He was drunk, also high as a fucking kite. He came into Sarah's house, attacked her. She managed to lock herself in her bedroom and called Raina. We called nine-one-one and got to her as soon as we could, man. He busted down her door. Hit her. Twice. Cops showed up and hauled him off."

"I'll fucking kill him! Where the hell is she now? Shit!" I can't think straight. I'm pacing back and forth across this small-as-shit hotel room, over seven hours away from her.

"She's with us, so calm down. She's okay."

"I'm on my way."

"Liam, man, she's good. She's finally asleep right now. So just leave in the morning, like you planned. No sense in driving through the night."

"I said I'm on my way. We'll be home as soon as we can."

It takes all the energy I have not to throw this damn phone across the room. He fucking attacked her? What the hell?

"What's going on?"

"Damn it, Cole. Daniel came to Sarah's tonight. We gotta go, man. I'll drive."

"What the hell did he want?"

"He attacked her. He hit her twice. Bruises. She's got bruises from that fucking asshole, and I've got to get to her, like, yesterday."

"Let's get the hell out of here then. But I'm driving. Get your bags."

The worst feeling in the world is knowing you're so far away from someone you love and not able to get to them. Seven and a half hours. That's how long I'll have to replay that shit over and over in my head until I can get to my girl. I've never wanted anything more in my life than to be with her right now.

I'll be home soon, baby. I won't ever leave you again.

THE DARKNESS of night begins to fade away, the light of the morning emerging as we make the last leg of our journey home. We're nearly to Zane's house and this last fifteen minutes is beginning to feel like fifteen hours. I'm antsy and can barely sit still.

"Liam, man, we're almost there. And for God's sake, don't run in Zane's house like some superhero, vigilante asshole. She's gonna need soft and calm."

"Who the hell are you and what have you done with Cole?"

"Shut up. I know women. I got their shit dialed in, man, and I know exactly what they need. Never had an unsatisfied woman leave my bed before."

"Honestly, Cole, I don't know how you do it," I say, shaking my head in utter confusion. "How you can be so smart and be such an idiot, all at the same time. Must be some kind of superpower."

"Hey, I've had lots of women comment on my powers. I think you may be just a bit jealous, if you want my opinion."

"Oh, yeah. That's definitely it."

The moment we pull into the parking lot of Raina and Zane's apartment, my stomach rolls and the anger bubbles up inside. My fists clench and I'm finding it difficult to calm myself down.

"I'm tellin' ya, bro. Calm. Just be calm. She'll be fine, she's a strong girl."

If he only knew the whole story.

"Yeah."

Before Cole even gets the car in park, I'm out the door and making my way to the apartment. Zane opens before I can even knock and tells me he was watching for me. Sarah is still sleeping after waking several times through the night, and he didn't want me to disturb her.

Looking over his shoulder, I see her. There she is, lying peacefully on the sofa, wrapped in a soft blanket, her head resting on a fluffy white pillow.

My angel.

Quietly, I walk toward her. I see the soft rise and fall of her chest that lets me know she's sleeping soundly. When I look to see her thickly-lashed eyes closed, I also notice two bruises on her face and my blood goes from hot to boiling in three seconds flat.

I'll kill him.

Unclenching my fists, I remember Cole's advice...soft and calm. Stealing a deep, calming breath, I carefully sit on the floor beside her, reaching out and using my fingertips to brush away a few strands of hair from her face. Just touching her satiny skin helps to subdue my anger. The soft exhale of her breath on my hand brings me some comfort. Staring at this beautiful woman, I take her all in, and let that image of her make its way deep into my heart, so that I will always remember that it's me who needs to protect her, who needs to be here for her. Those bruises will fade in time, but my need to protect her never will.

Looking over my shoulder, I see Raina standing right next to Zane. Tears in her eyes.

"You love her," she states.

"With every last breath."

I'd like to point out that never in my life have I ever cried over a woman. Then again, never has a woman ever touched something so deep inside me before.

"She needs you, Liam. She's going to try to push you away, you know. She's going to pull out her stubborn streak that's a mile wide and pretend she doesn't need anyone."

I chuckle and shake my head.

"I'd love to see her try. I won't give up on her, Raina." I think back to the night I took her home from the pub. God, she was lit, drunk as could be. However, she was alert enough to warn me not to hurt her. It was such a faint whisper that I barely heard it. "You have to believe me that I will never let her go."

"I do, Liam. Relationship-wise though, you'll be the first."

"And I'll be her last."

Chapter Twenty-Nine

SARAH

There's this faint touch on my face, so calming I never want it to end. My eyes flutter open, and the first thing I see is Liam. He's near tears and I know it's because of what I look like now. Bruises on my face and God knows what else because Daniel really did a number on me. I'm sure it's only a matter of time before he'll let me know he can't do this anymore. Too much drama, too much baggage from the past. And really, who could blame him. Men don't sign up for this kind of shit.

I try to shake the cobwebs from my brain. I finally fell into a deep sleep sometime during the night, but it certainly wasn't restful. Every time I'd begin to doze off, all I could see was Daniel, the outrage in his eyes and hear the hostility in his voice. In all the years I've known him, I've never seen him so antagonistic. Just goes to show that you never know someone completely. One more reason not to get too involved with people.

"I don't think I've ever seen a woman think so hard in all my life. My beautiful girl."

"Beautiful? I'm sure the bluish-purple bruises really add a

nice touch." My voice is flat, apathetic. Just how it needs to be.

I slowly sit up on the sofa, pulling the blanket with me to keep me covered.

"You know I could kill him for doing this to you," he whispers. "There's no fucking excuse for *ever* laying a hand on a woman. I couldn't give a shit what his reasons were. He's a dick, plain and simple. God, Sarah, I was so worried."

"He was drunk and high on something. He's never been violent in the–"

"Don't. Do *not* even attempt to brush over what he did to you by blaming it on the alcohol or the drugs. Men do not do that shit. Ever." Liam's anger is palpable. If Daniel were here right now, I'd be scared for his life.

"Liam, I can't think about me right now. I'm worried about Londyn," I say. "And, oddly enough, I'm worried about Sydnee. I have to try to talk to her because I'm sure she has no idea where Daniel even is. I'd rather Dad and Mom not find out, but I don't think there's any other choice but to tell them. They have to help Sydnee. What she did to me in the past was shit, and I'll never forgive her for it, but I have to help her, Liam. I have to go to her. As painful as that may be, I have to. And what Mom was trying to tell me in the hospital before I cut her off. She said Sydnee was having trouble. It was with Daniel. And I didn't even listen."

Chapter Thirty

LIAM

I'm calling bullshit, but I certainly don't say it out loud.

"You have to take care of you first. You're the most important thing, sweetheart. When I heard what happened, I nearly lost my mind." Thinking back to the phone call stirs up anger again, but I keep that shit locked down so as not to upset Sarah.

"What time is it? Wait...why are you here this early? You weren't supposed to be home until tonight."

"You didn't think I'd come for you when I heard? Zane called last night to tell me what happened. I couldn't get here fast enough."

Sarah looks quizzically at me, as if wondering why I came rushing home. Raina said she'd pull out her stubbornness and if I'm not mistaken, I'm thinking she's gonna pull it out now.

"You should go home. I'm sure you're tired. As you can see, I'm fine, so we'll just catch up later."

Yep. Called that.

Her attempt at nonchalance is futile. I'm not buying it.

Her first move is to try to get up off the couch and I know

as soon as she does, she'll walk away from me. Too bad for her, that's not happening because I've fought too hard for her to lose her now, and it sure as shit won't be because of Daniel. That asshole is more trouble than he's worth and if she thinks for one minute the shit I'm sure he filled her head with last night is remotely true, then she has another thing coming.

"No. You'll stay right where you are." My voice remains calm but firm. "Look at me, Sarah."

Her eyes are fixating anywhere but on me.

"Sarah, I said look at me." And when she finally focuses in, there is sheer determination in those two angry green eyes, but she will be no match for me.

"What did he say to you? He filled your head with all kinds of bullshit, didn't he?"

Sitting up, with her back against the sofa, she pulls the cover tightly for protection, which pisses me off because the last person she needs protection from is me.

"What he said was all true, Liam. I did lose the baby. His baby. It was my fault. I couldn't hold on to him and I couldn't hold on to my baby. His baby."

What in the ever-loving hell?

Before I can utter a word, Raina is sitting on the sofa right next to her, and she looks even more pissed than me. All I can think is she's in mama bear mode, and what she's about to unleash might not be pretty. I can only watch in awe.

"Sarah, I'm gonna say this once. So listen, and listen good. There is no doctor on this Earth that would ever place the blame on you for losing that baby. You did nothing wrong. You didn't drink, you didn't take drugs. There was nothing risky about your behavior at all. You. Weren't. To. Blame. If you don't believe me, start with the doctors here in town and go to every freakin' doctor in North Carolina. Tell them the story. And I can guarantee not *one* of them will place the blame at your feet."

Raina's voice is becoming more passionate as she speaks. Thankfully, she's telling Sarah exactly what she needs to hear.

"Daniel is a loose cannon and spewed crap at you that he had no right to. There is seriously something wrong with him, and you're right to be worried about Londyn and Sydnee. But we'll deal with all that later. Daniel's locked up and can't get to them. Right now, you focus on you. Sweetheart, you are worth so much more than Daniel or any other man has led you to believe. But I can't make you believe that. Liam can't make you believe that. Only you can do that.

"You just have to look at your life, look at all the wonderful things you've done. Even at eighteen, you were going to take on motherhood for the sake of that baby, and motherhood is some hard shit. You are an amazing teacher and every child that walks through your classroom door is a better person for having been there with you. Open your eyes, babe, and you'll see it."

I watch intently as it all starts to finally sink in. There's a change in Sarah's demeanor, her body language. She's starting to loosen up, her shoulders aren't squared off in tension, and there's just a hint of a smile. It was brief, but I saw it. I'm not entirely sure what part of that lecture that Raina just gave Sarah actually hit home with her, and I don't really care. I just need her to begin to believe in herself, to believe she matters. Because she's everything to me.

"You're right."

"Um...what?" Raina asks, drawing in her eyebrows, seemingly confused.

"I said you're right. I need to start getting rid of the head trash left from Daniel and start over. I won't let him get to me again. No more."

Hearing the determination in her voice makes me smile. She's gonna be okay. Might take a while, there may be a few setbacks, but she'll be okay.

"I do need to get to Sydnee, though. I think she's really in trouble. And that means Londyn is too. I won't have him hurting either one of them. It's time to put that behind me as well. She needs me."

"You and I will do that together. All in, babe, remember?" She gave me those words, *all in*, before, and she really thought she was, until Daniel tried to lay a damn guilt trip on her. "We'll go together to help her get out of whatever trouble she's in."

"Can I get up now, please?"

And we're back to sass.

All I can do is smile and wink.

"Wasn't me who just read you the riot act, babe. That's all on your bestie there."

"Don't use the word *bestie*, Liam. You're not twelve," she replies.

"She's right, Liam," Cole interrupts. Jesus, I forgot he was even here. That's the longest he's stayed quiet in the entire however many years we've been friends. "*I'm* twelve, remember. That's what y'all keep telling me, that I act like I'm twelve. Saying *bestie* is just all kinds of wrong, man. Even I don't say that."

"No, Cole, you don't. Thank God. Now if we could just improve on the rest of your communication skills, we'll be good," Zane replies jokingly. Leave it to Cole to lighten the mood.

Sarah leans into my touch as I glide my hands, starting at her temples and down over her pink cheeks, wishing like hell I could magically make the bruises disappear, make Daniel disappear. But I can't. What I can do is help her through the next hurdle. Helping her sister. I don't know what the dynamics of that relationship were before Sydnee slept with Daniel, but I do know Sarah barely speaks of her and avoids interacting with her at all costs. My guess is Sydnee's been good at hiding Daniel's behavior. But I think it's all about to come to a head as soon as we get to their house.

Chapter Thirty-One

SARAH

"Turn here. Second house on the right is Sydnee's." I'm not sure if my voice cracked when I said that or not, but I'm feeling nervous and slightly angry at the same time. This is the first I've been here in years and I'm upset it's under these circumstances. Liam's hand reaches for mine, which makes me feel significantly better. I'm so glad he is here with me. He's determined to make this thing between us work, so I'm trusting my instincts. And trusting him. He's never given me reason not to, in all these months we've been friends.

Liam pulls into the driveway and the first thing I notice is that all their cars are gone. I take a quick peek in the garage door windows and find it empty as well.

"Let's go to Mom and Dad's. I hope they're there."

Liam called the station before we left to find out the status of Daniel's arrest. At the moment, Daniel is still behind bars so we figure now is a good time to talk to Sydnee to help her figure out the next steps. I'm certain that if he acted out violently toward me, he's done it with her as well, and I can only pray to God Londyn was never on the receiving end of that behavior. Liam won't be the only one who'd like to kill him if he's touched a hair on that little girl's head.

Sydnee's car is parked beside Dad's in the driveway, and I breathe a sigh of relief.

We get out of the car and head inside, only to find Sydnee in tears, sitting at the kitchen table. Londyn is asleep on the couch, curled up with her blanket and stuffed polar bear I gave her a long time ago. Sleeping like an angel.

As soon as Sydnee and Mom see me, they both stand, rushing over toward us in the foyer. Sydnee wraps me in a hug and cries inconsolably.

"Oh my God, Sarah. I'm so sorry. He did this, didn't he? He attacked you?" she asks, carefully touching the bruises on my cheek. "He was so m–m–mad when he left. I had no idea he'd come after you. I haven't heard from him since he stormed out of the house." Her cries continue as she holds on to me. "We left and came here to stay last night. I'm not...I'm not going back."

When I finally get a good glimpse of her face, I see a Sydnee that is a shell of the woman she'd been. Her once vibrant and cheerful, and yes, dramatic eyes are now vacant and hurt. Her once shiny, thick hair is now dull and lifeless. What has happened to her? And yet, even after everything that's happened between us, I know she's still my sister, and I absolutely hate seeing her like this. Daniel has completely sucked the life out of her.

"He came to the house last night, blaming me for problems in your marriage. He implied that by me not telling him about the miscarriage, I'd caused a major rift in your relationship. I never expected he would have used me as a punching bag or I never would have opened the door."

"After all I've done, all that's happened, how are you even here?" she whispers hesitantly. "I hate what I've done, Sarah. You have to believe that."

"We can talk about all that later. I want to know what's going on. What has Daniel done to you? And please tell me he's never lifted a hand to Londyn."

Liam is being amazingly calm throughout the conversation we're having. Mom, Dad, Liam, and I sit at the dining room table with Sydnee and listen to her tell us about the change in Daniel over the past two years. While he's never laid a hand on Londyn, he's been anything but a father to her, never participating in raising this beautiful little girl. By the sounds of it, Sydnee has been a single mother, for the most part. She tells us of his emotional outbursts, his condescending remarks, and how he belittles her often, telling her she's fat and what a horrible mother she is, and how he regrets ever marrying her. He's never hit her, yet the years of emotional abuse she's endured has left her nearly empty. Had it not been for Londyn, she would have fallen apart completely.

"You need to file a restraining order against him, Sydnee," Liam states.

Dad speaks up right away, agreeing with Liam.

"The process has already started. Yesterday was the last." Tears begin to fall again as Londyn comes into the dining room, dragging the stuffed bear behind her, and crawling up onto her mommy's lap. She lays her head on Sydnee's shoulder while Sydnee holds on to her baby for dear life.

We all spend the next couple of hours talking and catching up. While Sydnee's actions years ago were ones I never thought I'd get past, I've learned so much about her and why she did what she did in just this little sliver of time. Getting over it won't happen overnight, and though she knows that, she has made it perfectly clear to me that she regrets everything she did, telling me she never meant for it to happen, and that she got caught up with him before she really knew what was happening. The biggest surprise was finding out about Daniel's gambling and drinking.

Sydnee and Londyn will be staying with Mom and Dad for now. They both feel safe here and with the restraining order soon to be in place, everyone feels certain they will be okay. Physically, anyway. It's going to take Sydnee a long time to come to terms with what she has suffered. Physical scars heal. Emotional ones can be carried around for life, like a ball and chain, always a reminder. I pray she gets some help, a good therapist, who can help her sort through her feelings and her fears.

And wow. Pot meet kettle. Huh.

As we all walk outside, I sweep Londyn off her feet in a huge hug, kissing all over her adorable face, before saying goodbye. She giggles and laughs like a little girl ought to.

"We getta stay at Mummum's and Pappy's, Aunt Sarah! We getta have a bunch of seepovers ev'ry night. And Pappy's makin' me panpakes ev'ry morning too."

"Oh, you're going to love staying here, my little Londyn. Pappy makes the best panpakes ever." I love the little slipups she makes with her words, and laugh when I repeat them right back to her. I've got plenty of time to fix those. For now, she gets to be little.

Sydnee pulls on my arm, stopping me before I get into Liam's car.

"There isn't anything I can say that'll excuse what I did to you. In a way, though, I'm glad it wasn't you who married him. I never ever want you to have to go through what I went through. Maybe I just deserved it," she says, half-chuckling. "Karma is a bitch."

"Never. Sydnee, don't even think that. No one deserves that kind of treatment. It isn't Karma. It was just Daniel being unstable and out of control. That's all on him."

"Do you think you'll ever forgive me?"

"We'll talk, Sydnee. I promise. We'll talk."

"I love you, sis."

"You take care of Londyn. I'll be back. I think she and I need some time to shop. She doesn't have nearly enough girlie stuff, you know."

Mom looks at me and smiles, wiping a tear from her eye.

We all laugh, and for the first time in six years, I'm starting to feel comfortable being around my sister and mom again. Forgiveness feels good.

Chapter Thirty-Two

LIAM

I t's been a week since the attack on Sarah, and in that week's time, her bruises have nearly vanished, Sydnee and Londyn are living full-time with Mr. and Mrs. Witten, and Daniel has been relatively quiet. The only peep we've heard out of him is a text to Sarah, apologizing profusely for how he attacked her. He blames the alcohol and the drugs, of course. He mentioned Sydnee, saying he was honoring the restraining order and was checking himself into a rehab program nearby that was court-ordered. That's the only way that piece of shit was staying out of jail. Of course, if I had my way, he'd rot in jail, so I'm sure he's glad I'm not in charge of the judicial system.

Sarah and I are at our favorite Italian place having dinner before we head to the pub. Cole and I are playing a few sets tonight and introducing two new original songs that we hope will be picked up by one of the artists Chrissie manages in Nashville.

We have another meeting with her; however, this time she'll already be in Raleigh, so she is driving to the pub tonight to meet Cole and me there. This will be the first time she's heard us in this environment, and we're both excited to share the new stuff. For whatever reason, Sarah doesn't talk much about Nashville or Chrissie, so I hope when she meets her tonight, things go well and they get along.

"Sarah, I've been thinking, and I'd like to take you home so you can meet my folks sometime. If you're up for it, that is. I don't want to rush you into anything. I mean, you'll get to meet Chrissie tonight. There's a lot of important people I want to introduce you to."

Sarah stops mid-drink. She puts down her wine glass, looking at me with a smile, which warms my heart. Dinner is finished and we're making short work of the wine that's left.

"I think I'd like to meet your parents. I know how important your family is to you. Maybe a little more time, for the bruises to heal completely, though? I'd hate for them to have to see me like this."

"What way is that? Stunning? Because that's how I see you, bruises or not."

"You might be just a bit biased, I think. But if it's all the same, I'd really rather wait another week or so. I want to be as comfortable as possible, and if I know the bruises are still visible, I'll feel uneasy and a bit too self-conscious."

"Whenever you're ready, babe. My sister is coming tonight, but she's cool. You'll love her, even more than Tatum, and I know you two got along well. I've explained about the bruises and told her not to even bring it up."

"Chrissie and your sister all in one night? Shit, Liam."

"There's nothing to worry about. Brooke is just...Brooke. Down to earth, laid-back. She's the last person to judge anyone. And Chrissie has this big important job with important, famous people, but you'd never know it. She puts her pants on one leg at a time like the rest of us. You'll see."

"Okay. If you say so."

"I say so. But right now, we better get going. Cole and I

have to set up and depending on his mood and his women, it can take a while." I lean in close to whisper in her ear, "And just so you're aware, tonight, when I get you home, I'll be claiming this body of yours. I haven't been inside you all week, waiting on you to heal, and I don't think I can take another night."

The slight hitch in Sarah's breath is a good indication she's turned on. Which is exactly what I need her to be. She can think about it for a while...delayed gratification and all that.

"Liam...um, we've got a bit of time. We could always take a quick detour. Maybe the office at the pub before your set?" she asks, winking and running her finger along my collar.

"Oh, shit. Look at the time. We need to get going," I say with a smirk, which earns me a punch on the shoulder and a heavy sigh.

I throw down some cash to cover the bill and take her hand, walking toward the exit.

"You'll pay for this, you know."

"Looking forward to it, babe."

Chapter Thirty-Three

SARAH

We arrive at the pub at the same time as Raina, and because Zane is tending bar tonight, she and I find our table near the front and make our way there. Once we order drinks from the server, I excuse myself for a quick bathroom break. My stomach has been in knots all night, and I know it's because this Chrissie person will be here to listen to Liam and Cole. Brooke, Liam's sister, is also coming to hang out with us and this will be the first time meeting her. Brooke hasn't been to see Liam and Cole sing in quite a while and because she has a night off, she decided to drive here to see him, and to meet me. Apparently, Liam's been yapping on and on about me, and she needed to meet me herself.

I barely make it to the bathroom in time before my stomach swirls with nausea and nearly everything I had for dinner comes back up. I hold tight to the railing in the stall for support as another wave hits, and whatever is left in my stomach makes it way up. Sweat beads on my forehead and my knees tremble with the strain.

"Jeez. What is wrong with me?" I say to no one in

particular. I don't know what it is about meeting Chrissie that has me such a wreck. Maybe she's prettier than me? When I see her name pop up on Liam's phone, I have to admit the jealousy monster rears its ugly head. She's obviously successful and rubs elbows with Nashville's elite. So yeah, she's kind of a big deal. My mind tries to wander off, making me think Liam would leave me for someone like her, someone he has things in common with. I'm trying not to let it go there, but that thought just sneaks its way in and it pisses me off. Residual trust issues from the past pop up again.

A splash of cool water on my face brings me back to focus. As I turn to walk out, a beautiful, but older blonde with piercing blue eyes and legs for miles, strolls in, nearly knocking me over.

"Oh, heavens. I'm sorry, hun. Are you okay?"

"Um. Yeah, I'm fine. Sorry about that? I'll just...get...get out of your way."

"Oh, goodness, no. It was my fault. Wait...are you Sarah?"

"Um. Yes. I'm afraid you have me at a disadvantage."

"Well, I'll be. You're prettier than Liam said you were. He's told me all aboutcha, ya know," she spews in her southern twang, making me sicker than I was just five minutes ago. Is she some bimbo he hooked up with? How old is she, and why would he tell this skank, this cougar, about me? Jesus, I can't get control over my emotions lately.

"Huh. That's nice. I've got to go find my friend. Nice to meet you..." I say quickly, attempting to sidestep her and hustle out the door.

"Chrissie. Chrissie Hamilton," she announces, holding her hand out to shake mine. "I've been working with Liam and Cole, getting some of their original songs out to a few country artists for recording. They are just amazing, right?"

"You're Chrissie?" I hate that I sound so confused, but she

is not *at all* what I had pictured in my mind. She's...older. Probably twenty years older than I imagined.

"Well, yes, honey. I am. I can't wait to hear Cole and your guy tonight. My husband was supposed to be with me but had to return to Nashville for an emergency business meeting. I hope the next time we meet, he'll be with me, so I can introduce y'all. Oh, he is so wonderful." When she says that, her eyes brighten and she smiles sincerely.

The diamond ring–or *rings*, I should say–on her left ring finger shine like a beacon and for whatever reason, my breathing returns to normal. All of a sudden, I'm happy to finally meet Chrissie.

"Then I can't wait to meet him. I'll have a seat for you at our table near the stage, if you'd like."

"That would be amazing, hun. I'll be out in a jiffy."

Raina is waiting at our table with drinks, along with Liam's sister, Brooke, when I return and I'm glad my stomach has calmed down somewhat. They both howl with laughter when I tell her about my run-in with a very married Chrissie, and how I thought for sure she was some skank that hooked up with Liam. This is the first time I've met Brooke and telling that story makes me seem like some kind of insecure teenager.

"Wait till you see the diamonds. I'm not sure how she holds her hand up with the size of those suckers."

"Oh my God, Sarah! You thought Liam was hooking up with her?"

"Damn, that sounds bad, doesn't it? These last few days, it's like every single emotion that can be wrung out of me has been. The other day, I cried when a little boy in my class stood up and read his poem aloud, and it wasn't even sad. You must think I'm some kind of crazy."

Brooke laughs, putting her hand gently on my arm.

"Not crazy, no. Unless it's crazy for Liam, then maybe so." She winks at me and I can tell she and I will be great friends.

Just then, I see Chrissie exit the bathroom and motion for her to come to our table, pulling up another chair for her. The server takes her drink order and hustles over to the bar. I introduce her to Raina and Brooke and before long, the four of us are laughing and having a great time. Turns out, Chrissie has a very pleasant personality and is extremely kind and generous, offering to let us stay at their place in Nashville, if we ever want to tag along with Liam and Cole. She assures us, with six bedrooms, there will be plenty of space. My house has two, so six? Yeah. That'll be plenty of room for Liam's entire family.

Sexy and charismatic. That's my man. He is on stage singing an original he and Cole wrote about a man who tries to convince a woman she is everything to him. That he is so deeply in love with her he'll never let her go. I get lost in his eyes. Those fiery, tense eyes that are gazing into mine, because I know this song is about me. Through his music, he's telling me what he needs me to know.

I have fallen so in love with this man. Right at this moment, chills come to life and work their way through my entire body, causing a shiver. Before I can shake them off, a single tear falls to the table, my shoulders visibly relax, and I nearly melt when I see the very honest, candid smile he gives me.

LIAM AND COLE talk at length with Chrissie after they finish both sets, and just the smile on Liam's face indicates that the conversation is going as he had planned. If she likes the two originals they sang tonight, that would be four songs of theirs that may possibly be recorded, and I couldn't be prouder of him.

"Babe, you ready to go? I'm just about worn out."

The guys are finished packing up their gear, and the bar is cleaned and closed for the night.

"Let's get out of here. I have kind of a funny story to tell you on the way home," I say as we lock up and walk toward Liam's car. "It's about Chrissie."

"Chrissie? Oh, shit, Sarah. You didn't think..."

"Oh, yes I did. I'd never met her before, Liam. I had no idea." I laugh just thinking about the first meeting with her. I can only hope she never finds out, or I will be mortified.

I proceed to tell Liam the story and he finds the entire situation just as humorous as Raina did.

"I know. She caught me completely off guard, and I didn't think. I'm sorry I thought that. She really is a genuinely nice person. Offered to let us stay at her house if we ever tagged along to Nashville with you."

It seems I've been staying more and more at Liam's house as the weeks go on, which is totally fine by me because sometimes our schedules don't mesh at all, and the only time I get to see him is in the morning or when he comes home late from the bar.

"Bathroom's yours, babe," he says, pulling me close and eating me up with a kiss.

"Don't fall asleep, stud. I'll be right back." My hand grazes his cock, and I feel it twitch when I shift to walk into the bathroom. A little grunt passes his lips, and I know he'll be more than ready. "Remember. You're playing me like your guitar tonight, right? Plucking and strumming a perfect tempo. Mmmm," I moan. "So, yeah. I'll be right out."

His smirk is back and he winks, smacking my ass...again.

I no sooner enter the bathroom than my stomach begins to

churn again, and, for the second time tonight, the contents of my stomach are emptied. In reality, all that would be left is some wine and the crackers and cheese tray we ordered to share.

Liam must hear me because he's standing right there at my side while I kneel in front of the toilet.

"Jesus, honey, are you okay?"

"Just wait for me out there. You don't want to be in h–"

I can't even finish the sentence before I'm sick again. Liam grabs a washcloth and runs it under cold water, then gently places it on the back of my neck while he holds the hair back from my face. My hands are gripping the edge of the toilet seat, and when my stomach settles, I rest my head on my arms, breathing out a sigh of relief.

The cold cloth feels refreshing when he strokes it across my forehead and dabs it again on my neck.

"This is twice tonight. I think one of those kids shared their germs." I stand and brace myself, turning to Liam. "Let me wash my face. I feel gross."

"What do you mean, *twice*? Were you sick earlier?"

"Well, yeah. I thought it was nerves. You know, meeting Chrissie and your sister and all. They're both important to you. But I guess not. I mean, I felt fine when I got to our table, and even had a glass of wine and some crackers and cheese. I didn't feel sick then at all."

"I'll stay right here with you while you change, then we'll get you to bed."

And he does just that. He helps me get my PJ's on and stands like a guard dog at the ready when I wash my face. It's so domestic feeling. Like we're husband and wife, and for the first time in, well, forever, the thought of that kind of rela-tionship doesn't scare me at all.

"Can you just hold me?"

"Come here, baby. You feeling okay now?"

"Much better. Especially with you here. Thank you, Liam. I love you."

"Love you too, babe."

The tiredness hits me quick and hard, and I know I'll only last a few minutes before I fall sound asleep.

Chapter Thirty-Four

SARAH

he smell of freshly-brewed coffee and frying bacon
hits my nose the moment I open my eyes, still
exhausted after ten hours of sleep. And the next
moment, I'm in the bathroom, sick again. This is not good.
This can't be happening. Not again.

Once my stomach settles, I lean back against the bathroom vanity, knees up, head down, and try to sort in my
mind how this happened. I chuckle, albeit a brief one, and
I'm reminded that I know exactly how this happened. Liam
and I had sex. Liam and I love sex, and we have a lot of it.
And the pill isn't one hundred percent. But seriously, is it the
universe conspiring against me that I would be in the one-
percent of women on the pill who actually get pregnant? I
take those little suckers every day at the same time. I only
missed one. *One* pill. One time.

One teeny tiny little pill, and now there's probably a teeny
tiny little human growing in my uterus. Panic sets in and my
breathing accelerates; my pulse is pounding. I can't do this. I
can't go through this again. Tears come full force, and as
soon as I try to stand and run, strong arms surround me.

"I've got you. You're okay."

"Liam. Liam, I think I…"

"I know, babe. I know what you're thinking. And it's okay, sweetheart."

"Oh, God, Liam. I can't," I cry. "I can't do this again."

His strong hands hold on to me, rubbing up and down my back, his lips firm on the top of my head. It's somewhat comforting, but then my mind goes back to six years ago and I break down again, nearly collapsing in his arms.

"Sweetheart, you need to breathe. Come on, babe. Breathe with me. Slowly." His voice is quiet and calm, his fingertips caressing my shoulders. "In through your nose and out through your mouth. Take it slow," he whispers in my ear, never letting me go. "That's it. A few more slow breaths. I've got you, baby. I'll always have you."

Chapter Thirty-Five

LIAM

S arah finally relaxes enough and I carry her back to my bed, holding on to her, letting her know I'm here for her. Her sobs and tears are damn near enough to break me.

I think I can pretty much confirm now what I thought last night.

She's pregnant.

First thing this morning, while Sarah was still asleep, I called Brooke, who broke out in a scream when I told her Sarah might be pregnant. Her best friend is a nurse so I wanted to give her friend a call. After a brief conversation, I actually felt a whole lot better. She told me that if Sarah is in fact pregnant, the chances of another miscarriage are very small. It's much more likely she'll be able to carry a baby to full-term than to miscarry again. Although she's going to be a hard sell, even with the facts.

But, first things first. We need to confirm she's actually pregnant.

I can't help but smile, thinking that Sarah could be pregnant with my baby. Unfortunately, this could be a nightmare for her.

Leaning down, I kiss her on the forehead, only to discover she's asleep again. At least she's settled right now. Her breathing is slow, but even, and her long, thick lashes are resting on her cheeks. With or without make-up, Sarah is the most beautiful woman I've ever seen.

For a brief moment, I think how beautiful a baby girl would be if she looked like her. Flawless, creamy smooth skin, with big, shiny green eyes, and dark curls. She'd be a stunner, the most gorgeous baby in the nursery, no doubt. And I don't even think that would be a biased opinion.

I ease out from under a sleeping Sarah and go to the kitchen, to clean up the mess and put the cooked bacon in the fridge.

Deciding to let Sarah sleep a bit, I grab my guitar from the spare bedroom. Right now, lyrics to a new song are all jumbled in my head, so I also snag a pen and my notebook to jot them all down.

My mind drifts when I'm standing in the doorway to the spare room, looking around at what could possibly be a nursery. I know I'm way, way ahead of myself, but the visions of this comfy room being a place for our baby makes me happy, most likely because it's with Sarah. So, I decide to sit in here to write and play, finding inspiration in the fact that I might be a father very soon.

IT SEEMS like I've been at this for hours. It's so easy for me when the thoughts are there and the words are flowing. I've written nearly one complete song and the ideas for a second are scratched on the next blank page of the songbook.

Out of the corner of my eye, I notice movement, and when turn to look, I see Sarah leaning against the bedroom door, her hand splayed across her stomach. Almost as if she's protecting our baby. I keep forgetting that we really don't even know for sure she's pregnant, but it seems as though she's almost certain. She's in one of my shirts, and it practically comes to her knees. There is sadness in her eyes that I hate seeing there. She pushes off the door, walking slowly toward me. All I can do is stare at my gorgeous girl, eyes tired and red, hair piled on her head with a few tendrils framing her beautiful face.

"I'm scared," she whispers as she sits on the ottoman, facing me in the chair. "And I'm so sorry. This is all my fault."

"Wait a minute. Last I checked, it takes two people to make a baby, and to be honest, we had a damn good time doing it. But sweetheart, we're not even sure yet that you're pregnant."

"I missed a pill." Her head is down, and her voice is so soft I almost missed it.

"What?"

"I missed a pill. But Liam, I swear to you, I didn't do this on purpose. I swear I didn't. I would never do that to someone on purpose, like Daniel said. And you know I don't...I mean, I didn't even want to get pregnant." She's talking faster and faster, starting to panic again.

"Stop. Stop right there. Deep breaths again, babe."

Jesus, if I have to hear that man's name again, I may just scream. It's like he's some kind of fungus that I can't get rid of, try as I might.

"Sarah, I know you didn't get pregnant on purpose. I know that."

"You do?"

"Jesus. Yes, I do." I put down my guitar and pull her over

to my lap, framing her face with both of my hands. "Sarah, if you're pregnant, I am completely, one-hundred percent okay with that. I love you." Shrugging my shoulders, I continue, "I would've liked to ask you to marry me first, but it's okay. This is not a hardship for me. I'm twenty-seven years old. And if I get confused on all things baby, I'll ask Cole for advice."

"Oh my God you wouldn't." She laughs. It's a beautiful sight, I might add.

"No. I wouldn't. But it made you smile, and that's what I wanted to see." I tuck Sarah's head under my chin and rub her arm, trying to help with the anxiety she's feeling. I take a minute and let the scent of her hair fill my nose. It's the same scent on my pillowcase that I wake up holding after she's gone to school.

Shit. I hope I never accidentally spill that little tidbit to Cole. He already tells me I've lost my balls.

"Let's go to the drugstore today and get a test. We'll get three if you want, just to be sure. We'll find out together, and if you are pregnant, you will be fine."

"How do you know that? You don't know that for sure. What if I lose this baby too?"

"I don't know for sure. Sometimes you have to take a chance. It's a risk, but baby, virtually every good thing in life is. What I do know is that you're young and it's much, much more likely that you'll carry a baby full-term than have another miscarriage. Just because you had one, doesn't increase the chances of having another one."

"Who told you that?"

"Brooke's best friend is a nurse. I called her this morning. You're tired, you're sick. I just put two and two together and kinda figured it out myself. And I have to tell you," I whisper quietly in her ear, "the vision I have of you pregnant with my baby is damn near the sexiest thing I can think of."

Her eyes get misty again and her hands reach for mine.

"I'm so scared. I've already had wine and I know you can't drink alcohol when you're pregnant. What if that does something?"

"That little bit isn't going to hurt a thing. Just don't have any more. And if you don't calm your fine ass down, I'm gonna smack it," I say with a smile. "Now, get the ass up and let's get ready to go. We'll get some drinks you like and saltines while we're out."

"You're a smart man, Liam Reynolds, my ass smacker extraordinaire."

"And you're a beautiful woman, Sarah Witten, my little worry-wart."

THREE PREGNANCY TESTS and two panic attacks later, we discover that Sarah is pregnant. And God love her, she's handling this the absolute best she can. It isn't possible for me to completely understand her fear, but I'm doing everything I can to try to alleviate it.

Last time, she was so young, so stressed. This time she has me, and I can guarantee I will be sure she's taken care of the way she should be. She told me I didn't have to go to every doctor's appointment with her.

I told her I did.

She told me I didn't have to redecorate the spare bedroom as a nursery.

I told her I did.

She told me I didn't have to buy her a new maternity wardrobe.

I told her I did. And not only did I buy her a new maternity wardrobe, I bought a diamond ring as well, and I'm waiting on the perfect opportunity to ask her to marry me. I'm thinking the sooner, the better.

So, I think she gets it now. I'm all in. And there's no one in the world I'd rather have a family with than her.

Chapter Thirty-Six

LIAM

I t's been eight weeks since we confirmed Sarah is pregnant. Some days have been calm, and other days, it seems she's in a downward spiral of emotions...similar to being on a roller coaster...ups and downs, twists and turns, and a few loops along the way. There have been times when I've felt like my head was spinning trying to catch up. Yet, it's one of the things I love most about her. Remember I said Mary Poppins or Satan? Yeah, that's pretty much it. Wouldn't have it any other way.

The reports she is getting from the doctor are wonderful, and she's progressing with this pregnancy beautifully. With each visit, she relaxes more and more, and is beginning to enjoy this wonderful time in her life.

Mom and Dad are on their way to visit, and we're all headed to the Italian place where Sarah and I had our first *official* date.

I'm stunned when I see her coming out of the bedroom, where she spent the last three hours getting ready. Fucking gorgeous. The loose-fitting top camouflages the tiny baby bump that has developed. One thing is for certain, her tits aren't tiny bumps. So far, that has been the best side effect of Sarah's pregnancy.

Without even looking in her room, I know all her clothes are strewn across the bed, and most likely, six pairs of shoes are out of their boxes and laying on the floor. She's nervous, I get it, and she wants everything to be perfect when she meets my folks. What she doesn't understand is that it's all those little imperfections that make her absolutely perfect to me.

She stares at me with a reserved look in her eyes.

"You're stunning," I whisper, pulling her close to me and running my finger down her cheek. "My beautiful girl."

As sensual and physical as Sarah can be in the bedroom, she shocks me when she stands on her tiptoes and places the gentlest, most tender, kiss on my lips. Nothing, absolutely nothing, could be better than this right now. This is my Heaven, right here on Earth.

"We better get going," I say, Sarah still in my arms. "Mom and Dad are already at the restaurant."

"Liam, what are they going to think of me?" I feel the soft exhale of her breath.

"What will they think? They will think you are the most beautiful woman in the world and that you make me ridiculously happy. That's what they'll think. They've already heard so much about you from Brooke and Tatum. They've wanted to visit and meet you sooner. But with Dad being sick, they just couldn't."

"I do love you. It wasn't easy to admit that, but I do."

"I know, baby. Resistance was futile, though," I say with a smile. "You didn't stand a chance."

I'm blessed with a shy grin and her gentle lips on mine one more time before she backs away, grabbing her coat.

❧

Dinner was amazing, as usual, and Mom and Dad fell in love with Sarah. How could they not? All through dinner, she was completely herself...stubborn, gentle, kind, funny, sometimes quiet, most of the time not. Everything that made me fall in love with her in the very beginning.

I squeeze Sarah's hand as we walk into Sam's a short while later, so Mom and Dad can catch Cole and I performing a few sets tonight. It's been a long time since they've been able to visit me here as busy as they've been with work, and with Dad getting over a nasty case of the flu. Our usual table near the small stage is open, so I situate Mom and Dad there with Sarah. Zane and Raina are at the bar, ready to watch the show because it's going to be a special one. It'll be the one performance that will always be the most memorable.

Cole and I hop onstage as he introduces us to the audience, although most everyone here knows who we are.

"Liam here has a special song he'd like to start off with tonight for a very special woman. Sarah, can you come up here?"

Instantly, her eyes search mine for an answer. She points to herself and mouths, "*Me?*"

"Honey, how many other special Sarah's does Liam have? Get your sexy ass up here, babe. We got shit to do."

A complete lack of filter is Cole's specialty, so why I'm surprised at his comments, I have no idea.

I pull a chair over close to me as Sarah winds her way through the crowd and onto the stage. Zane and Raina are standing at the bar, Raina's back to Zane's front, more in love now than ever before. Looking over at them, I see a thumbs-up from them both. All of a sudden, I'm nervous as shit.

Taking the microphone, I begin.

"Ladies and gentlemen, I have a special song I'd like to

dedicate to this beautiful woman sitting here beside me, most definitely my better half. And I'd also like to announce that we're going to have a baby." Before I can even continue, whoops and hollers rise up from the crowd. There are tears in Mom's eyes, a smile on her face at hearing the news her first grandchild is on the way. "Yes, there's a future little Liam on the way. Or maybe a Liamette. Don't know yet."

"Dude, if you name your baby Liamette, we're through. That's not even funny, man."

Chuckles and laughs can be heard coming from the crowd as Cole gets his two cents in.

"As I was saying, we're going to have a baby. And I have a very important question I need to ask. But before I do...Cole, let's play the song."

Cole begins picking the strings and strumming, and I join in after a few notes. With my heart and soul in every word, I sing "Marry Me" by Train, to the woman I want to marry, the very best part of me.

With tears in her eyes, Sarah watches as I lay down my guitar and pull out the perfect diamond ring from my jeans pocket. Kneeling down on one knee in front of her, I hold up the ring, watching it catch the light and sparkle like the light in her eyes. The ring that she will wear for the rest of her life. A life with me by her side.

"Sarah, you are, by far, the most stubborn woman I've ever met. You've challenged me in ways no one else has, not even my two sisters. And you've wormed your way so far into my heart, so deep, that without a doubt, you'll be there forever, and I couldn't be happier. I love every single part of you. Every smile, every tear, every breath, every heartbeat...I want them all for me. I've found my forever in you, baby. Will you marry me, Sarah?"

Sarah's right hand covers her mouth in surprise as I take her left hand, sliding the ring on her finger.

No words are spoken, but I see all I need to in her eyes.

She stands, throwing her arms around me. I'm just hoping a nod of the head counts as a *yes*.

Chapter Thirty-Seven

SARAH

Six months later...

I can't get up. I can't even get up out of the damn tub. It's like I'm an overgrown, water-retaining sea cow.

"Liam!" Oh shit. I didn't mean to be quite that loud.

"What? What's wrong?" he asks, breathless from running in from outside.

"I can't get the hell out of this tub. All I wanted was a damn bath. One simple thing, and I can't do it."

"Ah, there's my gentle, peaceful baby mama."

"Liam, I swear if you don't help me out of this tub now, I'll..."

"...you'll what? Honey, there's no room to pull me in, so I'll take my chances." He's such a shit. Cracking jokes about this.

"You do realize you'll have to go to sleep sometime, right?"

Obviously, that was funny to him because he throws his head back, laughing, all while lifting my pregnant ass from the tub. And if that wasn't sweet enough, he wraps me in the oversized towel I had to buy to dry my overly large, pregnant body. He rubs my protruding belly and sings a lullaby to our baby while he dries me off.

Okay, so I won't murder him in his sleep.

"Mrs. Reynolds, you are, by far, the most gorgeous pregnant woman on this planet. Not only was I lucky enough to knock you up, but to persuade you to marry my sorry ass? I couldn't be happier."

"Mr. Reynolds, just when I think you couldn't be any more romantic, you go and spew shit like that."

"Baby, you're worth it."

"Liam..."

"Yeah, baby?"

"I think we have a bit of a problem."

"Oh, sweetheart, I can fix anything. What's wrong?"

"The water running down my leg isn't from the tub."

"You should pee in the toilet, Sarah...oh, shit. Did your water just break?" Here's the part where my normally calm, reserved man begins to hustle around the bedroom, grabbing the suitcase he packed two months ago, swearing that it can't be time already, while I stand in the bathroom, wrapped in a towel, water running as if it's coming from a wide-open spigot down my leg. He takes off down the hall, and then sprints back, taking my hand to hustle back down the hall with him.

He turns and simply stares at me.

"You aren't even dressed yet, Sarah. What are you waiting for?"

"Christmas, Liam. I'm waiting on Christmas. What in the hell do you think? And why the hell did you drag me to the door when I was still stark naked in the bathroom? Focus, Liam!"

I hurry back to the bedroom and quickly throw on a jersey knit maternity dress and the biggest underwear known to man, with two large pads to try to catch the fluid.

Liam piles towels on the passenger seat of the car and helps me in, tossing my suitcase in the back seat.

I shoot off a short text to Mom and Sydnee, and their return texts come quickly. They're on their way. My heart swells a bit when I see how excited they are. It's been a long road getting our family back on good terms, a lot of arguments and tears, but sometimes you just have the let the past be in the past and move on. The relationship with my sister is stronger than it's ever been. Forgiveness is a wonderful thing.

Sydnee, however, says she will never forgive Daniel for what he put her through. He still goes to meetings at the rehab center, and is trying to clean himself up, but the damage is done. Supervised visits with Londyn is the only kind of relationship Daniel will ever have with his little girl. The divorce was finalized yesterday.

"You were a million miles away, sweetheart." Liam leans over the console, seemingly calmer now, to kiss me. And he kisses me like he always does, like he'll never get enough. The entire way to the hospital, he holds on to me. That's what he does. He holds me, calms me, and keeps me grounded. We joke with each other, take care of each other, and love each other more than I thought two people possibly could. He's my solid, the one man who made me believe I deserved to be happy.

And we're having a baby.

Epilogue

LIAM

It's been three months since Sarah gave birth to our beautiful baby girl, Isabelle, and four months since Raina and Zane had their son, Zander. Tonight, we're all sitting around our backyard fire pit for a quiet Saturday night in, having a few drinks and roasting marshmallows. Mom and Dad stopped by for a while, but decided to leave when I announced that Mom was hogging the babies. She just laughed and handed Isabelle back to me...where she belonged.

Cole and Samantha have been taking over the bar on Saturday nights so we can have some family time together. We all seem to find that odd considering she can barely stand to be in the same room with him. At least that's what she *wants* us to see anyway. Cole and I still play at the bar occasionally, and I see the longing in her eyes when she's looking at him. Whether she realizes it or not, I know that look. I used to look at Sarah the same way.

The bar continues to do well, and we've got a bid in to buy the empty lot alongside the bar to open an outdoor section, which would include an additional bar and tables, and a killer fire pit. It seems like a perfect complement to what we've done inside.

We still meet with Chrissie in Nashville once a month. Writing songs and hearing them brought to life by some of the best musicians and singers in the business is a very humbling experience. The passion and emotion they put into our lyrics and stories is nothing short of amazing. Seven months ago, we learned one of our songs was nominated for Song of the Year. Even though we didn't win, it was a true honor to be nominated with some of the best songwriters in the country.

Strangely, Cole seems more than satisfied with this arrangement. I thought for sure he would consider going out on his own, to try his hand at recording. He sang at my wedding and ever since then, he's seemed different in some way. Certainly, he's still the fun-loving, ever inappropriate, seemingly immature guy he's always been, yet somehow, he's settled. Don't know what happened, or *who* happened, but he's my best friend, so whatever, or whoever, makes him happy, is what I want for him.

Right now, my hand caresses Isabelle's fuzzy little head as she's cradled into my chest, and my fingers trace small circles around her chubby pink cheeks while I sing to her, and to Zander, both wrapped in blankets to ward off the chill of the night air. Pink and blue blankets. The color of cotton candy. Looking at my wife as I think this, I can guarantee she has never been more beautiful, more amazing, than she is right now.

She gave birth to our baby, my Isabelle, and I chuckle when I see her little eyes fighting to stay open. She's got her momma's stubborn streak, which means I'm in for an exciting eighteen years with this one. But I wouldn't have it any other way.

There's nothing like this in the world. My little Isabelle. The night she was born, I made a promise that I will always hold on to her, just as I will her mother. They are mine to care for, and love and protect. They will always be my girls.

The End

Also by Olivia Stephen

Acknowledgments

A huge thank you to so many people who continue to help me on this amazing writing journey. First and foremost, a massive, over-the-top thank you to my family. I am so blessed to have a wonderful support system cheering me on and encouraging me to continue this dream of being a writer.

A big bear hug to my wonderful friends, Pam, Susan, Debbie…my phantom sisters. Miles may separate us, but friends forever, right? Also, many, many thanks to my new-found friend, Valerie. Your humor, kindness, thoughtfulness and all-around compassion have helped me in ways you'll never know. I just hope you always stay comfortable in your tent.

More thanks than I know how to give to my editor and beta readers. Jenn, Melissa, Kristen, Valerie and Jeannette, your guidance and feedback helped me to craft a story that I am proud to publish. You were gracious enough to stop what you were doing to help me each and every time I messaged. I am so thankful to have your support and friendship. My story would not be what it is without you.

Huge hugs to my reader group and ARC team! You all really do rock and it has been humbling to know so many people are looking forward to reading my stories. I appreciate your encouragement and enthusiasm, your humor and kindness.

Thank you to all the bloggers and readers for your excitement about Liam and Sarah's story. I deeply appreciate each and every review you left for this book, and for every time you shared their story.

Finally, and most importantly, thanks be to God for His never-ending grace and love.

About the Author

Olivia Stephen was born and raised in the mountains of Western Maryland and still resides there with her husband and two children. She is a teacher/literacy specialist, an avid reader, a wine lover, and enjoys trips to the beach with her family. Hold on to Her, Only Her Series, book 2, is Olivia's second full-length novel.

You can find more information on upcoming novels or follow Olivia Stephen on social media here:
www.facebook.com/groups/oliviasrockstarreaders

facebook.com/oliviaspage

instagram.com/oliviastephenauthor66

goodreads.com/AuthorOliviaStephen

amazon.com/author/oliviastephen

bookbub.com/authors/olivia-stephen